Romance Unbound Publishing
Presents

The Abduction of Kelsey
(formerly released as: Claiming Kelsey)

Claire Thompson

Edited by
Donna Fisk
Jae Ashley

Cover Art by Kelly Shorten
Fine Line Edit by Kevin Gherlone

Print ISBN 9781493761203
Copyright 2013 Claire Thompson
All rights reserved

Chapter 1

A dark, fierce power coiled inside him like a snake ready to strike. His hand was on her throat. He could feel the pulse of her lust beneath his fingers. His cock was hard as steel as he guided it into the wet, greedy grasp of her cunt. She moaned.

"Yes, that's what I need, James."

He pulled back, teasing Kelsey with the head of his cock, drawing out the moment as he stoked the flames of her passion.

"Please! Please, James. Fuck me," she begged.

She wrapped her strong legs around his hips, pulling him deeper into her. She gripped hard on the red satin ropes knotted around her wrists. "All these weeks sitting at my desk with you only a few feet away—it's been torture, James. I dreamed that someday you would take me into your arms, into your bed. At last I'm here with you. Don't make me wait any longer, James. Not a second longer."

The satin rope melted away and Kelsey reached for him, slipping her arms around his neck as she covered his face with tiny kisses. Her cunt spasmed around his cock like a thousand perfect fingers. "Don't ever let me go," she panted. "Promise me,

James. Promise me I will always belong to you, and you alone."

She shuddered beneath him as he swiveled and thrust deep inside her perfection. "Oh! Oh, oh, oh!" Kelsey cried in her throaty voice. James' balls tightened. Lightning shot through his shaft, exploding in a thunder of passion…

James lay still for a long moment, his hand wrapped around his wilting cock until the thud of his heart slowed. He opened his eyes, dismayed to realize he'd just ejaculated on his clean sheets, completely forgetting to grab the washcloth he kept by the bed when jerking off. He sighed heavily and rolled away from the sticky mess. He would change the sheets in the morning before work. He reached for a pillow and pulled it against his chest, nuzzling the edge of it. "Good night, Kelsey, my darling."

Loneliness moved over him suddenly, shrouding him in its dark, relentless embrace. Clutching the pillow tighter, James closed his eyes and waited for sleep.

~*~

"He stares at you. I've seen him watching you when you aren't looking. It's kind of creepy."

Kelsey laughed, shaking her head as she thought about her boss. "Aw, he's harmless, Jenny. I actually think he's kind of cute, in a nerdy sort of way. So serious. So proud of being a team leader. It's endearing."

Jenny shrugged. "I guess. He never looks at *me* that way." She took a bite of her sandwich and chewed contemplatively. "You're probably used to guys staring anyway. Every guy in our department has his tongue hanging out when you walk by."

The guys at Kelsey's new job were nothing to write home about, though she had gone out a time or two with a couple of them. Sometimes she thought she wasn't entirely over Adam, though she knew breaking up with him had been the right thing to do. College sweethearts, they'd stayed together over the years out of habit and convenience. Adam was like a familiar old blanket, but as Kelsey grew older, she found herself wanting more than familiarity. She wasn't ready to drift into marriage and slip into motherhood and find twenty years later that her life had somehow passed her by.

Life had to hold more, and she was determined to find it. Moving to the city, getting her own place, finding her own way—it had been exhilarating. She had made a fresh start, a clean break from the past. The last thing she wanted was to get involved with someone new. "I'm not looking for a relationship right now," she told Jenny. "I was with a guy forever back home. I like being single."

"I like it too, I guess," Jenny said, though her tone and body language belied her. "Still, if the right guy came along…"

"He will," Kelsey said reassuringly. "You're smart and funny and beautiful. "

"Ha," Jenny retorted. "And fat. Don't forget fat."

"Stop it. You're fine," Kelsey insisted. Jenny was in fact quite lovely, with thick, dark hair, clear skin and large blue eyes, but she *was* overweight, Kelsey had to admit. "But you know," she continued, "I was thinking about joining that health club near the bank. They're having a special on the membership. We could do it together, if you want. Be workout partners."

Jenny shrugged noncommittally. "I don't know. Maybe." She glanced at her watch and stood from the park bench. "We better get back to the office. Bennett's a stickler for punctuality."

~*~

James Bennett liked his job. He was a vice president at a large commercial bank, admittedly one of dozens of VPs at the firm, but still, it was nothing to sneer at. He had worked his way up from a lending officer in the mortgage department to special assets analyst. He found he didn't really care for the marketing side of the business. He didn't like pounding the pavement in search of new accounts, or schmoozing with strangers in an effort to procure their business. It suited him far better to work with numbers and documents, which didn't require him to smile and shake hands all the time, or pretend he cared about a client's new baby, their golf game, or the redesign of their office space.

Special assets was a euphemism for bad debt—loans the bank had already written off, but which loan officers still tried to restructure and collect. While good at the marketing end of the business, these loan officers relied heavily on the analyses of the clients' sales data, market share and financial structure provided by the special asset analysts. Last year James had been promoted to team leader in the corporate special assets, with responsibility for thirteen loan analysts. At the age of twenty-nine, this was no mean feat.

His life was full, with hobbies and exercise on the weekends, and a satisfying career. He hadn't even realized he was lonely until the day *she* appeared. Since the day Kelsey Rowan had applied for a job at the bank four months ago, James' world had been turned upside down.

She'd already passed the first interview hurdles with human resources when James was called down to meet her and conduct the second interview, along with the head of the department, Bob Reynolds. They were each given a copy of her resume and the results of the initial interview, but nothing had prepared

James for the sight of her when she appeared in the door like an angel just fallen from the heavens.

She had worn a high-necked silk blouse beneath a tailored navy blue jacket and matching narrow skirt. With her hair pulled back, sensible, low-heeled pumps and gold studs in her small, pretty ears, she'd presented during the interview as the very picture of professionalism, though James had immediately sensed the deep sensuality and passion barely hidden just beneath her conservative exterior. She had all the necessary qualifications for the job, including a business degree from a good university, and two years experience at a small bank in her home town. Though James would never have admitted it to a soul, he would have hired her if she'd been a high school dropout who'd never set foot in a bank. He would have hired her just so he could look at her.

The room that housed the analysts was nothing special. There were two vertical rows of desks, with cubicle half-walls separating one from the other to offer the illusion of privacy. James sat at his own much larger desk at the front, like a teacher in a classroom, though there was no chalk board behind him. He'd moved a more seasoned employee out of the front desk so he could place Kelsey there, and thus have an unobstructed view of her beautiful face, which he could observe in profile as she clicked away on her computer.

It wasn't just her beauty that captivated him, though she was lovely by any measure, with her tumbling, shiny red-gold hair and pouting red-lipped mouth, not to mention her slender body, shapely legs, and the hint of luscious breasts beneath her suit jackets and high-collared blouses. It wasn't just that deep, throaty voice—the voice of a jazz singer in a 1940s nightclub—or the way she seemed to pay such full and complete attention when he explained something to her, her clear green eyes fixed on his face as if nothing else in the world mattered but him. Yes, all those things contributed to his feelings, certainly, but it was something else—something that words couldn't quite capture—that had drawn him so utterly to her.

It was as if the two of them spoke a secret, special language. A language that didn't require words or prior knowledge to understand. While he knew it was corny in the extreme, he thought of it as a language of the heart. They were born for one another. She was his soulmate, and as odd it sounded even to his own ears, he'd known that from the moment he'd laid eyes on her.

For the first time since his promotion to head of his team two years before, James regretted being in a position of authority. Kelsey, understandably, was hesitant to get involved with her boss, and while James agreed with this stance in theory, it chafed at him nonetheless. He had considered getting her transferred to another department as a way to open the door that kept him from her, but found he couldn't bear the thought of not seeing her each and every day.

It had been hard to keep his emotions under wraps when she'd started having lunch with that asshole, Fowler Chandler, in accounting. What kind of stupid name was Fowler, anyway? Yeah, the guy was good-looking, James supposed, in an obvious, all-American dumb blond kind of way, but Kelsey deserved better. She deserved James, and he deserved her.

Happily, she'd soon tired of Chandler, and ate lunch most of the time with Jenny and Sarah, the other two women on his team. When Steve Hardin started nosing around her a little too persistently, James had been able to get the bastard assigned to an external audit, which got him out of the office for a few months at least. James had quietly seethed when Kelsey went out with the guy a few times after work, but she soon saw the error of her ways.

Meanwhile James bided his time as he contemplated when he'd make his move. For the time being, he contented himself with quietly, discreetly keeping his eye on Kelsey. Sometimes at work she would look up suddenly and their eyes would meet. Her shy smile radiated through him like liquid sunlight, and he would feel himself tumbling into her soul. That one moment of connection would be enough to see him through the day and to fuel his fantasies at night.

James had never taken the contractual mid-morning break before Kelsey's arrival, feeling that, since he was part of management, it showed a lack of professionalism. Since Kelsey had appeared, however, he had pushed these qualms aside, pulled into the break room by an invisible tether that bound Kelsey and him together. Though he rarely actively joined in his subordinates' conversations during these breaks, he kept his ear cocked for Kelsey's sexy, husky voice and drank in every word, no matter how mundane the topic.

One morning as James pretended to read his paper at a small table near the group, he was extremely annoyed by the way Frank Lease kept monopolizing Kelsey's attention with pictures of his stupid new puppy. Talk about an obvious ploy. James was pleased to see that, while she was pleasant and polite as always, Kelsey didn't seem terribly interested.

No — she was waiting for the right person.

She was waiting for James.

Just as he would wait for her, biding his time until the moment was right. As he lay in bed at night, cock in hand, Kelsey in his mind and heart, he thanked his lucky stars he hadn't made the mistake of marrying Emily Brookes. Unlike Kelsey, Emily had been too superficial to appreciate what he'd offered her. She had lacked the vision or imagination to understand how powerful true love could be.

To think how he'd groveled and pleaded for Emily to take him back. Recalling it now still left him sick with humiliation. She had cut him to the bone with that restraining order, but, as his mother had been fond of saying, everything happens for a reason.

After the breakup, James had promised himself he would wait until he found the right girl—a kindred spirit who understood that true love was all-encompassing and for life. Emily's betrayal had been the best thing that ever happened to him, as it left his heart free for Kelsey.

Now he just needed to find a way to let her know they could be together, even if he was her superior at work. Soon, soon, he promised himself, he would find the right moment to make his move. Then he would make all his dreams, and hers, come true.

~*~

The moment came sooner than he'd expected. It was the last Thursday of the month, and the crew was going out for their usual monthly happy hour excursion. James suspected the tradition had evolved for Thursdays instead of Fridays because his colleagues saved their Fridays for their real friends, but he had kept this perhaps uncharitable speculation to himself. James always forced himself to attend this event for at least a few minutes, aware he needed to be seen as accessible by his staff. Today, however, was no hardship, as Kelsey was also going. She'd glanced at him, smiling shyly after she'd told Anna Green, who sat just behind her in the office, that she would be joining them for a couple of beers that evening.

The rest of the day passed with agonizing slowness, the minutes inching forward like hours as James waited restlessly for five o'clock. There were seven of them going to Sal's Pub that evening, and they all walked together to the elevator and rode down to the lobby. James stood beside Kelsey, keenly aware of the fresh scent of her shampoo, and her shoulder lightly touching his arm in the crowded elevator car.

Once at Sal's, they were ushered to a large booth near the bar by the waitress. James was deeply annoyed when Mark pushed his way past James and plopped down beside Kelsey.

James consoled himself by sliding into the opposite side of the booth so he could at least face the girl of his dreams. Their knees were nearly touching beneath the table. If he'd dared, he could have reached over and touched her. The thought sent a jolt of electricity to his cock. Kelsey chose that moment to look up at him. As she graced him with her angelic smile, he *knew*, in his bones, that there was something between them. And tonight was the night they would make it real.

It took all his self-control not to warn Mark to keep his hands, his dirty thoughts and his eyes to himself. He had overheard the bastard talking about Kelsey in the men's restroom to Albert from accounting, unaware James was sitting in a stall.

"You seen the new girl? She's hot, man. I think she's into me."

Albert, bless him, had laughed. "You think every girl in this place is into you, Mark. What's Beth got to say about that?"

"My wife's interested in a three-way," Mark had claimed, though James, who had met the tight-lipped, perennially pissed-off Beth, highly doubted this.

They ordered pizza and two pitchers of beer. Jackets were discarded and ties loosened as the pitchers were emptied and filled again. Mark kept refilling the mugs of the three women at the table, though his attentions were clearly most focused on Kelsey, which annoyed the shit out of James. He decided he would quietly see about getting Mark transferred out of his department, even if he had to lie to get it done.

A few of the party left after the pizza was gone, and then a few more, until only James, Mark and Kelsey remained. James glanced pointedly at his watch. "It's nearly eight. Won't your *wife* be wondering where you are?"

Mark started to deny this, but just then his cell phone chirped. He glanced at it with a scowl, but took the call. Though he turned away from them, James could still make out his words. "Yeah, honey. Long day at the office, but sure, I'll be home soon. Yeah, I won't forget the bread and milk. Okay. Yes, okay. See you soon."

He swiveled back toward them with a rueful grin. "Guess I'll leave you single folks to it. Duty calls." He slid out of the booth and reached into his jacket. Pulling out his wallet, he extracted a few bills and dropped them on the table. "See you tomorrow."

Once he was gone, Kelsey pulled out her cell phone and glanced down at it. "Wow, I didn't realize it was so late. I have to be going too. I don't want to get stranded downtown after the last bus."

This was the moment, his cue, and, heart pounding, he took it. "I could give you a ride. My car's parked in the garage at the end of the block. It's no trouble." He held his breath.

"Oh, I couldn't ask you to do that," Kelsey said. "But a ride to the bus stop would be great." Her cheeks were flushed, her emerald green eyes bright. She brought a hand to her face, pushing away the loose strand of hair that had sprung from her French braid.

James realized he'd been staring, and he tore his gaze away from her to focus on the bill the waitress had just placed on the table. "I think I had a few too many," Kelsey said with a laugh. "How about you? You okay to drive?"

James glanced up from the cash he'd been counting, thrown on the table by the others as they'd left, which totaled about two-thirds of what they'd owed. He didn't care. He was with Kelsey! He was going to give her a ride to the bus stop, or, if he could convince her, all the way to her apartment.

"Me?" James offered a confident smile. "Sure, I'm fine. Let me just settle up this bill and I'm good to go."

Kelsey reached for her purse. James stopped her by placing his hand over hers. Oh god, her skin was so soft. "This one's on me, okay?"

She looked as if she was about to protest, but he caught her gaze in his and smiled gently. She pulled her hand slowly from beneath his and nodded. "Okay. Thanks. That's really nice of you, James."

James. He loved when she said his name. It sounded sexy in her mouth, like the promise of something more.

She sidled from the booth and turned to face him with a smile. "I'll just pop to the ladies' room, okay? Then we can go."

"No problem. I'll be waiting." James watched her walk away, drinking in the sight of her small but shapely ass as she glided like a geisha through the crowd. He refused to entertain a sudden niggling thought that she might not come back. Clearly she'd stayed late just so they would be the last two at the table. It was up to him, as the man, to make the next move.

He was waiting by the table when she returned. She'd reapplied her lipstick and smoothed back her hair. Her cheeks were still flushed and her eyes were shining. Her suit jacket was flung over her arm, and she'd opened the top two buttons of her blouse. James' fingers itched with the sudden desire to push her down against the table so he could claim her then and there. He shook away the image, hoping she wouldn't notice his sudden erection in the dim light of the bar.

He dared to place a hand lightly on her lower back as they pushed their way through the loud, drunken throng. It was a welcome relief to breathe the air outside, in spite of the fumes from a nearby bus. They walked in companionable silence to the car garage and James exercised every ounce of self-control to keep from reaching for her hand, or worse, pulling her into his arms.

Not yet, he warned himself. *Not yet.*

He felt lightheaded and almost reckless, and realized he, too, had had too much to drink. But so what? It only gave him the added courage he needed to make his move. Because tonight was the night. He was sure of it.

When they got to the garage, he led her to the small elevator that would take them to the top floor where he always parked. At this hour the place would be nearly deserted. As the elevator lurched upward, again he exercised all his self-control to keep from pressing her against the wall and kissing her.

As they walked through the empty garage toward his car, James clicked the button on his key fob to unlock the doors of his car, which flashed its lights in greeting as they approached. "I wish you'd let me take you all the way home. I don't like the idea of you waiting for a bus at this hour. The crazies come out at night, you know."

"Well, if you're sure it's not too much trouble," Kelsey said hesitantly.

"It would be my pleasure," James assured her, already imagining her inviting him up to her apartment. They would share a nightcap. She would smile shyly at him and lift her face for a kiss. When their lips touched, they would both know beyond a doubt that they belonged together as man and wife.

As they approached the car, Kelsey gave him her address and directions to her place, not that he needed them. The garage was empty and silent, save for the clacking of her heels against the concrete. The moon had risen and was shining in through the wide slats in the walls, casting a pearly glow over everything. Kelsey stood by the car like a shimmering angel.

James hadn't meant to do it, but somehow he found himself pressing Kelsey gently against the car, his hands on her shoulders. He dipped his head, unable to stop himself, the need to kiss her suddenly overwhelming him. A small voice whispered to wait, but James could wait no longer.

"Hey!" Kelsey twisted from him, turning her head sharply away. "James! Stop it. What're you doing?"

"What I've wanted to do since the moment I saw you." He tried to pull her back into position.

"James, cut it out. You're drunk. Look, I can just take the bus—"

James came suddenly to his senses. Holy shit, what the hell was he doing? His timing was off. He was going to blow this before it had begun. He tried desperately to backtrack. "Please forgive me. I lost my head for a second. You're right. This isn't the place. I—I got carried away. You're just so beautiful, Kelsey."

He realized Kelsey was backing away from him. She wasn't smiling. No, if anything, she looked horrified. Horrified! Like he was some kind of sex fiend or ax murderer or something. What the fuck? After all they'd shared? All the secret glances, the knowing smiles? What about tonight? She'd waited, along with him, until they could be alone at last.

Yeah, so he'd jumped the gun a little, but it wasn't like he'd whipped his dick out in the parking lot or anything. What was her problem?

She began to shake her head. "Look, I'm sorry if we got our wires crossed or something, but I'm not interested in you in that way, James. You're my *boss*. And anyway, I'm not looking for a relationship right now. Let's just forget this happened and..."

Her mouth continued to move, but James could no longer hear the words. The blood was roaring in his ears. He felt like he was going to explode. Rage hurtled through his loins and his hands clenched into fists at his sides.

This couldn't be happening. She couldn't be like the rest of them—just another prick tease, another fluff ball with nothing in her head or heart. How could he have gotten it so wrong? He brought his fists to his chest and pressed hard. His heart felt as if it had collapsed in a hard, tight ball in his chest.

Without realizing what he was doing, James reached for Kelsey. He grabbed her arms and pulled her toward him. "James! You're hurting me. Let go!"

He didn't let go. He dragged her back to the car and managed to pull open the passenger door, while still keeping her in a tight grip. He shoved her into the car and slammed the door. He pressed the lock button on the key fob while he sprinted around to the driver's seat. She was still trying to get the door open when he pressed the child lock button that only he controlled from the driver's side. Kelsey wasn't going anywhere.

Still blind with rage and grief, he started the engine and gunned the gas. Skillfully he maneuvered the car rapidly down the spiraling exit ramp toward the ground floor as if his life depended on it. Kelsey pawed at his arm while he drove. "Let me out!" she screeched. "James, what are you doing? Stop the fucking car!" She fumbled in her purse and pulled out her cell phone. James grabbed it from her hands and threw it in the backseat.

Keeping one hand tight on Kelsey's arm, James drove as quickly as he dared down the city streets and onto the highway that led to his home, thankfully only ten minutes from the office. A vein pulsed at his temple, beating time to Kelsey's caterwauling. Somehow he made it to his driveway.

He let go of Kelsey long enough to use the garage door remote that was clipped to his sun visor. He slid the car into the garage and pressed the button again to close them off from the world.

James turned to the beautiful, trembling girl beside him. His heart was pounding, his cock throbbing at full erection. He felt more alive than he ever had in his life.

Chapter 2

Kelsey grabbed for the door handle, wrenching it hard in her effort to get the damn thing open. Her fingers fumbled ineffectually with the lock.

Beside her, James threw his door open and raced around to the passenger side of the car. Acting purely off instinct, Kelsey changed her strategy, reaching wildly for the lock button. But James held the key, and Kelsey nearly fell out of the car as he jerked the door open. He dragged her from the car. As she tumbled out, her jacket and purse fell from her arm and she lost a shoe.

Unaware or indifferent to this, James yanked her through the door and into the house. This couldn't be happening. It just could not be happening.

Breathlessly, Kelsey cried, "James, please, James! Whatever you're doing, you have to stop. This is crazy. I know you don't want to hurt me." But did she know that? Kelsey tried to jerk out of his tight hold, but he was strong, much stronger than she would have thought. "You're drunk. You don't know what you're doing. Please," she entreated, "I promise I won't call the police if you'll just—"

"The police?" James' face was a mask of incredulous anger. "How dare you? After all we've been though together! You have no idea..." He pressed his lips together and angrily shook his head.

"What, don't tell me you'd rather be with that prick, Fowler Chandler, is that it? Don't think I don't know about him, and Steve and Frank, too. What other poor slobs have you been leading on? How many other hearts have you casually stepped on and ground into the dirt?" His grip tightened on her arms. "Well, you picked the wrong person this time, you bitch!"

"James!" Shock and panic bloomed into stark terror as James jerked her along through his kitchen and into the living room. He threw her roughly onto a sofa. Her other shoe fell to the carpet. Kelsey tried to slide from the sofa to the floor with an idea of scuttling away from him, but he was too fast for her.

He fell on top of her, one strong hand closing over her throat. He squeezed hard and she began to choke. She clawed at his hand with both of hers, but it was like pulling against iron. "James! No!" she tried to gasp, but it only came out as a squeak. She felt a steady, throbbing pressure building behind her face and her lungs ached for oxygen. Jesus god, was she going to die like this? Why? Why, why, why was this happening?

James released his grip just enough for her to draw a tremulous breath of air into her burning lungs, but he kept his hand around her throat. He unbuckled his pants with the other and pulled his cock out of his underwear. A new spurt of adrenaline hurtled through Kelsey as she realized what he must be intending, and she jerked and twisted hard in the man's grip.

She brought one knee up hard into his groin. He grunted and fell away, giving her the chance to roll from the sofa. As she struggled to get to her feet, he fell on her again, this time flattening her on the carpet with the full weight of his body.

"You bitch!" he snarled.

Kelsey started to scream, but her cries were cut off abruptly by a hard hand clamping over her mouth and nose. James loomed over her, his eyes wild, spittle on his lips. "Shut up," he hissed. "Shut the fuck up! You asked for this. You know you did. It could have been wonderful. We could have had it all." His voice cracked and tears filled his eyes, but then his gaze hardened once more.

He kept her pinned beneath him as he jerked her skirt upward and ripped down her pantyhose and underwear. She struggled hard beneath him and managed to dislodge his hand from her mouth. Again operating off pure instinct, she closed her teeth on the side of his hand and bit down as hard she could.

James shouted, "Damn it to hell!" He backhanded her hard across the face and Kelsey gasped in shock and pain. Then he was on her again, pushing his hard, thick cock between her legs. His shaft was like a knife plunging into her and Kelsey screamed. James cut off her cries with his hand, which clamped again over her mouth and nose.

He groaned as he pushed deep inside her. "I didn't want it like this, Kelsey," he gasped into her ear. "It wasn't supposed to be like this." He pummeled her, his cock like a steel rod thrusting inside her. "This is your fault. Your fault. Your fault. Oh, god!" He stiffened suddenly and then jerked spasmodically for several long, painful seconds inside her.

Finally his hand loosened from her face and Kelsey was able to turn her head to the side. She gasped beneath the man's deadweight. The air seemed thick and sticky and she found it hard to draw a breath. She realized she was crying in hiccupping, gulping little sobs. She tried to bring her hands to her face, but they remained pinned beneath James' heavy, inert body.

Finally he rolled away onto the carpet beside her. Though she still felt as if she were swimming through Jell-O, Kelsey tried to scoot away, but James caught her. He pulled her into his arms as he lifted himself into a sitting position. She tried to struggle against him with an idea to sprint from the room, but her rubbery limbs refused to cooperate.

James was holding her now in a tight embrace from behind, his arms wrapped around her torso as she sat between his legs, her back against his chest. She felt him begin to shake behind her and a strange sound came from his mouth. It took her a moment to realize it was a stifled sob.

He nuzzled his face into the side of her neck. "Kelsey. Oh god, Kelsey. I'm so sorry. I'm so, so sorry. It wasn't supposed to be like this. I didn't mean it. I swear." He began to cry in earnest.

Goosebumps prickled Kelsey's skin. James seemed to genuinely believe that she'd been into him—that they'd been flirting somehow at work and just biding their time until they could be together. The guy was out of his fucking mind. She had to get away from him, and fast.

Think of something, she ordered herself. But her mind remained blank as a white slate.

James pulled himself up, hauling her upright with him as he stood. He was no longer crying, though Kelsey wasn't sure if that was a good thing or not. Her pussy felt bruised and torn, and she felt the bastard's semen trickle down her leg. Rage bloomed in her brain, making her head throb.

Kelsey tried to twist in his grasp so she could face him. She willed her face into a smooth mask to hide the fury inside her. "James. You just had too much to drink. I get it. I just want to go home, okay? We'll both forget this ever happened," she lied. "Let's just put this behind us, all right?"

Far, far behind us, once you're in jail, you rat bastard.

James held her in place, not allowing her to face him. He pulled one of her arms behind her back and pulled it up hard. Kelsey cried out, wincing with pain. "I wish we could, baby," he said, his voice suddenly hard. "But you and I both know what's done is done." His voice softened. "I'll make it up to you, Kelsey. I swear I will."

He kept her arm twisted behind her back, though he eased off a little as he began to propel her through the room. He walked her in this awkward way to the doorway of what she saw must be his bedroom. Flicking on the light, he guided her toward the bed and fell onto the mattress, dragging her down beside him.

He drew her into a tight embrace, curling himself around her as she lay on her back in a shocked stupor. After a few moments, her eyes began to focus on the walls of room and a chill of horror turned her blood to ice water. Every wall held photographs, some framed, some blown up to poster size, every single one of them of her.

Holy. Fucking. Shit.

~*~

Kelsey's hair had come loose in the struggle and spread now across his pillow in a wild tumult of red, copper and gold, just like in his favorite fantasy, only now it was real! James inhaled deeply, closing his eyes as he savored the moment. She smelled so good.

A hint of perfume, the clean scent of soap, and beneath it the sharp, erotic tang of fear sweat. He couldn't deny her fear turned him on. It made him feel powerful in a way that was new to him.

He flashed back to the wild look in her eyes when he'd had his hand clamped over her mouth. He hadn't expected the fierce, intoxicating rush of power her fear had engendered. He couldn't deny it—he'd loved the struggle—holding her down while he ripped at her clothing and pulled out his hard, hard cock. It was like an incredibly hot porn video, the kind he'd jerked off to a thousand times, except this one was starring James Bennett and the sexiest, most desirable woman alive.

He had fucked Kelsey Anne Rowan. He had come inside Kelsey's hot, tight, perfect cunt. His cock stirred. He could fuck her again, right now, if he wanted to. And he wanted to. Oh god, did he ever. He growled and nuzzled his face against Kelsey's neck, feeling like a caveman, operating off primal lust and basic instinct.

She yelped in fear as he did this and tried to pull away, but this only made him clutch her tighter to him. Again he experienced that perverse, wild rush of power that turned the blood in his veins to fire. She was so small beside him. He could feel her heart beating fast and hard. He reached into her torn blouse, slipping his hand into the cup of her bra. Her breast was so soft. Satin and cream. His heart ached with the sweetness of it as he squeezed.

Though he knew he should feel only remorse and abject shame, instead he felt alive! The tears he'd shed back in the living room would be his last. With those tears, he had washed away any regrets. What was done was done. There was no rewind button on life, no wiping out what had happened. He'd changed the path of both their lives inexorably and forever with one single, wild act of passion.

James had reinvented himself in that one moment of unfettered lust. He was a different man. The old James was gone, and good riddance. The new James Bennett was a man who *took* what he wanted—who claimed his woman with sheer, brute strength. Yes! James Matthew Bennett was now that man.

Kelsey belonged to him. Whatever he'd dreamed of or planned up to this moment no longer mattered. Kelsey was his and he could never let her go. With that one brutal, thrilling act he'd made her his own. His cock pulsed with excitement and he tightened his grip around her.

"James, please, let me go."

"Shh." James moved to kiss her mouth but Kelsey turned her head away and he caught only her ear. He reached for her face and pulled it back to his. Holding her by the chin, he kissed her lips, forcing his tongue between them. She whimpered against his mouth and tried to squirm away, but he only held her tighter.

"Kelsey, you have to stop struggling. Don't you see? You're mine now. I've claimed you. You belong to me." His voice was deeper and stronger, and this pleased him. Did Kelsey notice the transformation? Did she realize she was lying with a new man? Did she feel his power? His passion?

"Ow! You're hurting me. James, quit it. Please. Please, just let me go." Kelsey began to cry, the sound ugly and guttural. Tears spurted from her eyes, which were squeezed tightly shut. Her mouth was open, the lips pulled down in an unflattering frown, and the tip of her pretty nose was reddening.

"Stop that," James ordered, pushing away the remorse that threatened his newfound he-man persona. He shifted a little and loosened his hold on her. Kelsey at once tried to squirm away from him. This wouldn't do. He couldn't very well hold onto her all night long.

Restraints. He needed some kind of restraints to hold her down. He had some rope in the basement, but that was too far away. He reached for his tie, amazed he was still dressed, if somewhat disheveled. Kelsey was still dressed too, save for the stockings and panties he'd torn from her body.

His cock was throbbing. Still keeping Kelsey pinned to the bed with one leg, James reached for his necktie and pulled it free. Lifting himself over her, he straddled her chest and grabbed her arms by the wrists.

Kelsey tried to pull away, but she was no match for him. Within a minute he'd managed to knot the tie around her wrists. He jerked them upward toward the wrought iron headboard.

"No, no, no! Stop it! Let me go! Let me go!" Kelsey struggled and twisted, making it difficult for James to get the ends of the tie probably secured over the horizontal bar at the top of the headboard. Frustrated and angry, he smacked her cheek. Kelsey gasped, her eyes widening with shock and pain. James smacked her again on the other cheek and then continued his task, this time managing to knot the ends securely around the bar.

He jumped from the bed and moved quickly toward his closet. He grabbed two more ties and hurried back to the bed. He jerked Kelsey's right leg toward the edge of the mattress. Working as quickly as he could, he wrapped and knotted one of the ties around her ankle and secured the other end to the bed frame.

He ran around to the other side of the bed, intent on doing the same with her other ankle. Though he pulled the leg wide, he realized the single tie wasn't long enough to get her tied down properly. She was kicking her free leg and shouting.

Frustrated and annoyed, James ran back to the closet and grabbed a handful of ties this time, along with a pair of socks. Returning to the jerking, howling girl on the bed, he unrolled the socks and stuffed one of them into her open mouth, muffling her piercing cries. He wrapped a tie over her sock-filled mouth and reached back to knot it behind her head.

Pleased with his handiwork, he returned once more to the other side of the bed. By knotting two of the ties together, he was able to reach the bed frame. He secured the end of the tie there, knotting it and giving it a tug to make sure it would hold.

He stepped back from the bed, breathing hard as he drank in the sight of his Kelsey, bound and gagged on his bed. He had done that! He was the captor and Kelsey was his prize.

As he regarded her, he decided the business suit would have to go. It would have been better if he could have stripped her before he'd bound her, but no matter. He loped into the bathroom, yanked open a drawer and pulled out the pair of barber scissors he kept there.

Kelsey was jerking and struggling in her restraints when he returned to the bedroom. Racing back to the bed, James grabbed the hem of her skirt and pulled it taut. Her eyes were wild and rolling as he held up the scissors, and she mewled with fear. Silly girl—did she think he was going to cut her?

"Stay still, Kelsey," James warned. "These scissors are sharp."

She stopped her struggling, though she was trembling, her chest heaving. The fabric gave easily against the sharp scissor blades, and he quickly cut away the offending garment, revealing her naked form beneath.

James drew in his breath with awe and delight as he gazed at Kelsey's spread pussy, the dark pink labia exposed beneath a tuft of downy auburn pubic hair. His cock throbbed. He would fuck her again. He would take his time and savor the moment. He would make love to her.

He put the scissors down on the bed and gripped the top of her already torn blouse. With a strong yank, he tore the blouse open, sending a small spray of buttons over the bed. The sleeves still hung on her extended arms but he was too eager to bare her breasts to worry about that now.

Grabbing the scissors, he carefully inserted the tip of one of the blades beneath the center of her bra. She squealed against her gag and jerked, nearly causing him to cut her. He tried again, this time getting the blade all the way under the bra between the luscious mounds of her breasts. He closed the scissors, cutting through the satin and lace with a satisfying snick, and the bra sprang free.

Oh god. Her breasts were even more beautiful than his endless fantasies. They were small and round, tipped with dark pink nipples the same color as her sweet cunt. Unable to resist, he leaned over her and drew one perfect nubbin into his mouth. He sucked it to a hard point and then teased it with his tongue. He released it, but only so he could suck the other one in kind.

Kelsey was whipping her head from side to side and whimpering behind the gag, her struggles pouring fuel on the fire of his lust. Christ," James murmured. "I have to fuck you again. I have to."

He jumped from the bed and pulled hurriedly at his clothing, kicking off his shoes at the same time. His cock sprang toward her, fully recovered, fully erect, its tip dripping with pre-come, his balls aching with need.

He fell onto her. She wriggled and jerked beneath him, but the silk ties did their job and held her fast. He wished he hadn't had to gag her, but he realized until he helped her to understand how things would have to be going forward, he had no choice.

Adrenaline and the thrill of the forbidden left James feeling as if he could conquer the entire world. Was this really happening? Kelsey looked so fucking hot, tied down on his bed, her green eyes wild, legs spread wide. She was more beautiful than he'd imagined, even in the most vivid dreams. Though he'd never planned it like this, he couldn't deny the dark joy surging through him.

James realized he was shaking, not from fear, but from the heady realization of what he was doing. In one act of dark passion, he had opened a door that could never be closed again. There was no going back.

He guided his painfully hard cock between Kelsey's legs, determined to be gentle this time. She was still sticky with his come and he slid easily into her heat. He groaned with sheer pleasure as her cunt gripped his shaft.

"Kelsey, darling," he gasped against her ear. "I've waited so long for this moment."

It felt so good. He could stay here forever, covering her sweet, naked body with his, buried deep in her cunt. He wanted to die like this, caught in the grip of her perfection. He began to move, swiveling and thrusting inside her. He pummeled her, his resolve to make love, to make it last, dissolving in the face of his blinding pleasure.

He realized one of his hands was on her throat. He squeezed, just hard enough to assert his dominance. He dipped his head and nipped lightly at her neck with his teeth. He was a god and she was his conquest.

All too quickly, he felt the rise of a climax shooting upward from his balls and along the length of his shaft. With a shudder and a cry, he released his seed for a second time. With a groan, he fell heavily against the bound girl beneath him.

He drifted for a while in a semi-conscious haze. Slowly he became aware of a muffled, mewling sound and realized Kelsey was crying again. His heart surged with pity and he pulled himself up. Rolling away from her, he leaned up on an elbow and gazed down at his girl.

He stroked her tear-stained face. "Shh, baby. Don't cry. Stop crying. It's okay. It's all going to be okay, I promise." She looked at him, beseeching him with those lovely green eyes. In that instant he forgave her for breaking his heart.

Smoothing back her tousled hair, he murmured gently, "Kelsey, sweetheart. Listen to me. If I take off the gag, you have to promise not to scream, okay? I know you're scared and confused, but things are different now. I understand you didn't mean to hurt me, and I forgive you. Together we're going to build a new kind of love—or rather, an ancient kind. The primordial and profound love of a strong man and the woman he has claimed."

She continued to stare at him as if she had no idea what he was talking about. No matter. He would show her what he meant. He would teach her. They had time. All the time in the world, now that she belonged to him.

Chapter 3

She was caught in a huge, sticky web that held her from all sides. The harder she jerked against her restraints, the more entangled she became. The spider was advancing, its huge fangs glistening with blood as it sidled toward her on the long, furry stalks of its legs. Kelsey opened her mouth to scream, but could only manage a strangled whimper. The spider opened its slathering jaws —

"Kelsey! Hey! Wake up. You're having a bad dream. Just a dream, sweetheart."

Kelsey's eyes flew open at the sound of a man's voice. What was a man doing in her apartment? As she came more fully awake she saw her boss, James Bennett, peering down at her with an expression of concern. His normally perfectly-combed hair was flopped forward onto his forehead and, as her eyes traveled down his bare chest, she saw he was naked!

All at once the horrifying, unbelievable events of last night blasted into her consciousness with the ferocity of a tornado. She tried to roll away from her abductor, but found her arms were numb, her legs still spread wide on the man's bed.

James continued speaking as if everything were nice and normal. "Wow, it's already six twenty. We'd better get up if I'm going to get to work on time."

Kelsey remembered now—he'd pulled that fucking sock gag out of her mouth finally, but had refused to untie her arms and legs, even when she'd pleaded with him. He'd draped his naked body over hers, one strong arm and leg keeping her pinned to the mattress. He'd fallen into a heavy, inert sleep, his breath on her neck, his snore in her ear.

She'd lain awake for hours, fruitlessly trying to work her way out of her bonds, hoping to slip from beneath the sleeping man and make her escape. After a while, though, she had given up, too exhausted to do much more than lie there in a stupor. And somehow, apparently, she'd eventually fallen asleep, only to be pursued by terrifying nightmares. At least those she could wake from.

"Did you sleep okay?" James asked in a solicitous tone.

"Did I what?" Kelsey blurted, incredulous. She glanced down at her body—there was a sheet over her lower half, but her breasts were bare. Her destroyed blouse still hung by the sleeves over her numb arms. "You have me bound hand and foot," she couldn't help adding. "If I slept at all, it wasn't well." She fought to keep her fury in check, remembering his rage the night before.

"Please," she begged instead, "untie me. Please?"

James regarded her solemnly for a long moment. "If I do, you have to promise not to do anything stupid like try to run away. Can you promise me that?"

Kelsey pressed her lips together to keep from screaming. What did this lunatic want from her?

He frowned, shaking his head. "What am I thinking? Of course you can't promise. Not yet. It's not fair of me to expect obedience when I haven't had time to train you."

Train her? What the hell?

James slid out of the bed. Kelsey closed her eyes to avoid looking at him. She heard him coming around to her side of the bed. She felt the give in the mattress as he sat beside her, and she whipped her head in the other direction.

She heard the drawer on the night table open and then close. "Kelsey. Look at me. Look at what I'm holding." His previously solicitous tone had taken on a hard edge, and Kelsey didn't dare to refuse him.

She gasped when she saw he was holding a gun, its muzzle pointed in her direction. She tried to scream, but her voice had died in her throat, and she only emitted a small, strangled squeak.

James kept the gun pointed at her. "I won't harm you as long as you don't give me cause. But you need to understand that I mean business. As long as you obey me and do what I say…" He let the incomplete sentence hang menacingly in the air.

Kelsey's heart was beating high in her throat. "Please," she managed to gasp, her voice sounding small and far away. "You're really scaring me. Please, James," she implored, "this has to stop. Let me up. Let me go home. Please, just let me go!" Kelsey was shaking so hard her teeth began to chatter.

"Hey, calm down. Stop it, Kelsey." To her vast relief, James put the gun down on the night table and reached for her wrists. He tugged at the knots for a few moments, and finally her hands flopped down from the headboard. For a moment she felt nothing, and a surge of panic hurtled through her at the thought that her arms were paralyzed. But after a few seconds, she felt them tingling to life. Another few seconds and the tingling became painful as the blood rushed back to her cramping arm muscles. She brought them forward over her breasts.

James, meanwhile, was busy loosening the ties around her ankles, and after a moment he lifted her into his arms. He carried her into the bathroom and set her down on the toilet. She stared mutely up at him.

"Go on," he said impatiently. "Use the toilet. Hurry up."

Kelsey realized her bladder was full, painfully full, in fact. She closed her eyes and concentrated on letting go in front of this madman. Finally her body relaxed enough to let her pee. When she was done,

James pulled her up from the toilet and pointed to the bathtub.

"Climb in. Go on. Move."

Though she would rather have showered, Kelsey welcomed the chance to bathe. She felt soiled from her head to her toes. She stepped over the side of the tub and sat on the cold porcelain, wrapping her still-tingling arms protectively around her body.

James reached to turn on the faucet, and warm water began to fill the tub. Bending over her, James lifted his hand and for a moment Kelsey was afraid he was going to strike her, but he only reached for a plastic bottle of liquid soap that sat on a narrow ledge set into the wall. He thrust the bottle toward her. "Clean yourself up."

Kelsey wasted no time, scrubbing herself vigorously to wash away the man's sperm and sweat from her body, though she couldn't wipe away the fresh memories of what he'd done to her. Rage bloomed inside her, and she tried to hold onto it. It felt better to be angry than terrified. She would have to bide her time to get herself away from this lunatic. She would have to get hold of that gun. She had no idea how to use a gun, but how hard could it be? She'd aim the damn thing at him and pull the trigger.

Could she actually kill a person, when her own life was at stake? Maybe she'd just shoot him in the shoulder or the leg or something. Then she'd call 9-1-1, if she could find a phone. Once she shot the bastard, she would find his car keys and get the fuck out of there as fast as she could.

She glanced at James as the tub filled. He was standing at the toilet, urinating without a trace of self-consciousness. When he was done, he moved toward the sink, where he began to brush his teeth, as if this were just another work day.

Work!

If she didn't manage to get out right away, the other loan analysts would notice her missing. But James had said he was going in to the office. Was he going to make up a story about why she wasn't there, or just feign ignorance? Jenny and Sarah had her cell number, but would they call or text? What would it matter if they did? James had thrown her cell phone in the backseat of the car.

Surely someone would look for her eventually, but who? She hadn't been in the city long enough to really set down any roots. She connected with people from home from time to time on Facebook, but it wasn't like she was on there every day. She regretted now that she didn't have a roommate—someone to miss her when she didn't come home at night. She regretted that she only checked in with her parents down in Florida once every six weeks or so.

It was chilling to realize there was no one to miss her, at least not right away. No one at all.

She stared at the broad back of the naked man standing near her. If only she hadn't dismissed Jenny's apprehensions about him. Jenny had been more right than she knew. James had not only had a crush on her, he'd been stalking her. He'd been watching her after hours, monitoring who she went out with, all the time harboring some crazy idea that they were meant to be together.

Why hadn't she realized any of this was going on? She would never have walked with him into that empty car garage if she'd had even an inkling of his twisted obsession. She shuddered to think how well he'd hidden it behind his tailored suits and bland smiles.

James whipped his head in her direction. His face, she saw, was half-covered with shaving cream. He gestured toward her with his razor. "You about done? When I'm finished shaving, you're done bathing, so be quick about it."

He turned back to the mirror. Kelsey's skin felt raw from scrubbing, but she still felt dirty and violated. She leaned back in the hot water, wishing she could somehow wash this whole nightmare away.

"Okay." James turned to her, wiping a trace of shaving cream from his face with a hand towel. "I'll shower when I get back. If you want anything to eat before I leave, you better hop to." He clapped his hands impatiently as if she were some kind of trained animal.

Not daring to refuse him, Kelsey hauled herself to her feet. He tossed a towel in her direction. She climbed out, wrapping it around her body. He walked out of the bathroom and into the bedroom. She followed, and her eyes moved toward his night table, and the gun resting carelessly on top of it. She measured the distance between herself and the weapon. If she sprinted fast enough...

The moment was lost as James strode toward the night table and picked up the gun. He waved it at her and gestured toward the bed. "Sit down and don't move while I get dressed."

Kelsey moved toward the bed, keeping the towel clutched around her body. She watched him as he dressed. He kept the gun in one hand while he pulled on his underwear and pants. He placed the gun on top of the bureau while he pulled on one of his perfectly starched white shirts and buttoned it, his eyes never leaving her.

To avoid his gaze, Kelsey looked around the bedroom, taking in the literally dozens of pictures of her hung so carefully on every wall. Some had been taken while she sat at her desk or in the break room. There were some of her eating lunch with the girls on a park bench, one of her waiting at the bus stop, one of her standing at the mailboxes at her apartment complex. Even more chilling, she recognized some from her Facebook photo albums. These were only visible to her Facebook friends, yet somehow he'd had access to them. What other parts of her life had he violated?

Her eyes returned to the gun, but James stood between it and her. Somehow, she had to get that thing before James left the house, as it was clear he didn't plan to take her with him.

James dressed quickly, transforming into the well-dressed, mild-mannered loan analyst she'd thought she knew. Her heart sank as he picked up the gun and slid it into his jacket pocket. "Stand up," he ordered. "Drop the towel and put your hands behind your back."

Instinctively Kelsey scooted back on the bed and away from him. James bent down and grabbed her roughly by the arm, pulling her from the bed and to her feet. "Damn it, Kelsey. Do what I say!" The towel fell to the ground. Still gripping her wrist, James reached for one of the neckties he'd used on her ankles.

Roughly he pulled her arms behind her back. Kelsey didn't dare struggle too much. James might just be insane enough to shoot her dead, in spite of his freaky obsession with her. He forced her arms up high on her back and she winced with pain.

"Please," she begged. "You're hurting me."

"Stay still and do as you're told, and I won't have to hurt you, Kelsey," he said, but to her relief he allowed her to lower her arms enough so that it didn't hurt. He tied her wrists so they were resting one above the other, her forearms parallel to the ground. When he was done, he knotted another tie around her neck and gave it a tug. "Come on. Let's get something to eat before I go. I won't be gone long. Just long enough to get our story in place at the office."

Kelsey stumbled along beside James as he pulled her by the makeshift leash. He led her into the kitchen and pushed her down onto a chair, one of two at a small table set against the wall. She perched on the edge of the seat, trying to keep her balance with her arms bound behind her back.

James was staring down at her with hungry eyes. She felt incredibly vulnerable, with her bare breasts thrust forward by her position, and she flushed with furious embarrassment beneath James' gawping stare.

Finally he tore his gaze from her and moved toward the counter. "Would you like some coffee?" His tone was scarily conversational. "Sorry, I don't have any cream. I take my coffee black. I didn't realize you'd uh, be staying over or I would have been more prepared."

Staying over? Was this asshole for real? Kelsey didn't reply, but James didn't seem to notice. He pulled two mugs from the cabinet and busied himself with the pot.

Kelsey sat numbly on the chair, desperately trying to come up with a plan. She had to get out of this surreal nightmare, but how?

James opened the refrigerator and returned with a butter plate and a jar of preserves, which he set on the table. He slid four pieces of toast into the toaster and then poured coffee into the mugs. "Two sugars, right?" He looked positively smug.

Kelsey wanted to scream. She wanted to spit in his face. She wanted to leap up and kick him as hard as she could in the balls. But her eyes were drawn like a magnet to the bulge in his jacket pocket, and she only nodded.

She watched as he slipped into the chair across from her and added sugar into one of the mugs, again apologizing for not having cream. He stood again when the toast popped up. In spite of her fear, the toast smelled good, and Kelsey realized she was starving.

She watched hungrily as James buttered the toast, wishing she could pick up her damn coffee mug and take a swallow, or better yet, hurl the contents in the bastard's face.

"You like jelly? It's apricot."

Kelsey nodded again. James smeared the preserves over a slice of toast. He held it to her mouth. "Have some."

She took a bite, savoring the crunch of the toast against the explosion of melted butter and apricot preserves, startled at how good it tasted, in spite of her predicament. James took a bite from the same piece and then lifted his coffee mug to his lips. After he drank, he lifted the other mug and held it close. Kelsey parted her lips as he carefully tipped some of the hot liquid into her mouth. It was strong and sweet, and though she missed the cream, it, too, tasted much better than it had a right to.

Thus he fed her, alternating bites with her, and sips of coffee, until all the food was gone. James glanced at his watch. "I better get going. I need to talk to Reynolds and get things settled with human resources. I won't be long, though. A couple of hours, max."

"You're going to leave me here alone?" Kelsey blurted, and then at once regretted the outburst. Better to be alone. Maybe she'd be able to escape in his absence.

James patted her shoulder. "Don't worry. You'll be perfectly safe. I know just what to do with you." He bent toward her and tugged at the makeshift leash around her neck. "Come on. No dawdling. We're going downstairs. I'll show you to your, uh, accommodations." He chuckled as if at some private joke. With no choice in the matter, and mindful of the gun still in the man's pocket, Kelsey allowed herself to be pulled upright.

James led her down narrow stairs into a finished basement that contained various pieces of expensive-looking home gym equipment. He pulled open a door on a room no bigger than a closet. There was a large dog bed on the floor, and nothing else.

"You'll stay here while I'm gone. That bed belonged to Sophie, my dear, departed yellow Lab. She died two years ago and I never had the heart to get another pooch. Good thing I saved the bed, though, huh? You can sit on it while you wait for me."

Kelsey stared at the dog bed, a few stray dog hairs still evident on the fabric that covered it. He wanted her to wait in a closet in the basement? Was he out of his fucking mind?

Of course, she already knew that yes, he was. Better in the closet than in his bed, with him rutting on top of her. "My arms?" she said. "Could you please untie my arms while you're gone?"

James pursed his lips, considering this. Finally he shook his head. "I don't think so. You'll be fine like that. The bonds aren't that tight, and I won't be gone long." He pushed her into the closet with a firm hand.

Before she could react, he slammed the door closed, plunging the tiny room into darkness. She heard the doorknob jiggling and then the sound of heavy footsteps receding as he climbed the basement stairs.

Miserably, Kelsey moved cautiously toward the wall, stepping gingerly onto the thick, spongy dog bed. She lowered herself carefully to her knees and let herself fall onto her side. The bed still smelled of dog, a warm, welcoming odor that brought back childhood. Tears rolled down her face and she sniffled.

"My god," she whispered to the dark. "What's going to happen to me?"

Chapter 4

"I must say, I'm quite surprised, Jim." Bob Reynolds ran a hand through his thick mane of silver hair, a serious expression on his tanned face. "Kelsey Rowan struck me as a serious young woman, not the flighty type at all."

James nodded soberly, ignoring the man's persistence in calling him Jim, even after years and countless requests to call him James. "I agree, sir. You could have knocked me over with a feather when I got her message this morning. I'd have at least expected a little notice, even if we didn't ask her to stay on for the full two weeks."

"Did she say where she went?" Reynolds pressed his hands flat on his huge, shiny desk. "First Savings & Loan's been trying to steal away some of our lending officers." He balled his hand into a fist and pounded his desk. "Damn it, did she take proprietary files with her?"

"No, no," James said quickly. "That was the first thing I checked, believe me. She didn't take a thing from her desk, not even her personal items. She just said she's quitting effective immediately and moving out of the state." He leaned forward conspiratorially. "I'm guessing it's something, uh, personal. You know, guy trouble. Or something worse. You never know these days. It's a shame though. She was starting to really contribute to the team. And now..." James drew in a deep breath and let it out as a long sigh. "Now, in light of the other news I have to tell you, it's especially unfortunate that we'll be understaffed." He pressed his lips together and looked down at his lap, blinking rapidly as if to fight away the tears.

"What?" Reynolds demanded. "What do you have to tell me? Is there something wrong?"

James drew in a deep breath, as if girding himself for what he was about to say. He looked up directly into Reynolds' pale blue eyes. "Um. Well, in a word, yes."

"What is it, Jim? More trouble with your staff?"

"No. It's, uh," James hesitated, and then plunged on, "it's personal. I guess I've been putting it off — using work as an excuse to keep from focusing on the possibility something might be wrong. I — I finally went to the doctor earlier this week when the pain just got too bad. I got the results of the lab work yesterday evening and it's really thrown me for a loop. It seems I have," he paused and swallowed hard, putting a brave face on it, "a rare kind of cancer."

"Cancer!" Reynolds exploded. "But you're so young!"

"Yeah." James gave a defeated shrug and, for extra effect ran his hand over his eyes. "My mom died of cancer. I guess," he let his voice crack, "I guess it runs in the family."

Reynolds had risen to his feet. He stepped around the desk and came to James, clapping him firmly on the shoulder. "You'll need a second opinion. Damn it, we'll fight this thing. When's the last time you had a vacation, anyway?"

Perfect.

"Gosh, it's been a while, sir. Work's been so busy and—"

"Damn it, Jim. That's part of your problem. Life's too short. Haven't you heard that old adage about all work and no play? You need to take some time off, man. Get that second opinion, rest up, figure out how you're going to lick this thing."

"But my staff—"

Bob help up his hand. "Forget about your staff. Forget about the damn bank. Take a week, two weeks, all the time you need. I'll talk to HR. We'll get that end sorted out. Your job will still be here when you get back, don't worry. Your number one job right now is to get better. Got it?"

"But my work—"

"No buts. Now get the hell out of here. I'll talk to your staff myself. Go on."

James stood, making a show of his reluctance. He felt almost guilty when Reynolds suddenly grabbed him in a bear hug and said in a strangled voice,

"Hang in there, Jim. You'll beat this thing. I know you will."

James drummed the steering wheel as he drove. His body felt light, his muscles taut with nervous energy. If he could have run home instead of driven, he would have been glad for the release. "I did it. I fucking did it!" he shouted over the pulsing beat of the song on the radio.

It had been so easy. Laughably easy. He shook his head as he thought about the way Bob Reynolds' face had crumpled with pity at James' mention of the word cancer. It was one of those words that made people turn away, not wanting to probe too much, not willing to ask the questions that might make them think about their own mortality. He hadn't even had to bring up the idea of sick leave or vacation — Reynolds had beaten him to it.

It felt odd to be driving in the wrong direction, whizzing past the three lanes of cars inching forward toward the skyscrapers in the distance. He hadn't been lying in that regard — it had been a long time since he'd taken any vacation, or even the occasional sick day. Shit, he could probably take off a full six months and still not use all his accrued time.

Not that he was going back.

There was no going back.

He could never let her go. No matter what threats he made or promises he extracted, he could never trust that Kelsey would remain silent.

The only way forward was together. Whether bound by hate or love, they were bound forever. For him, of course, it was love. He hadn't meant to force her, but the passion behind the act remained pure in its essence. He loved her. He had loved Kelsey Anne Rowan from the first moment he'd seen her face. It was as if he'd been waiting all his life to find her, though he hadn't known until the moment he saw her that he'd been waiting.

He wasn't foolish enough to think Kelsey felt anything close to love for him at this point. He would have to teach her about love. True love. The kind of love that made you willing to die for another person.

He pulled into his driveway and slid the car into the garage. "Honey, I'm home," he called out with a grin as he burst into the kitchen. Tugging at his tie, he pulled it from his shirt and draped it, along with his suit jacket, over a kitchen chair. He picked up the handgun from where he'd left it on the table. Pulling open the basement door, he thundered down the stairs.

Reaching the storage closet, he turned the lock in the doorknob and yanked the door open. Kelsey was lying on her side. Her eyes flew open as he entered the space and crouched beside her. Her bare breasts looked so luscious. He couldn't help it—he reached out and stroked the impossibly soft skin, his hand sliding to her nipple, which he rolled between finger and thumb. His cock strained in his pants.

Kelsey whimpered at his touch, her eyes swinging to the gun in his hand. He followed her frightened gaze to the weapon. "As soon as you can show me you aren't going to try anything stupid, we can put this thing away."

"I won't, I promise." He wanted to believe her. "Can you untie me?" she begged. "My arms are asleep." Her eyes were red, her cheeks streaked with tears, her nose running.

James felt a sharp pang of remorse at how he'd left her, but what choice had he had? "You promise? I don't want to have to hurt you."

She struggled to sit upright. "I promise, James."

James.

Even in her fear, she caressed the word with her throaty, sexy voice. *She* had never called him Jim.

He set the gun carefully on the floor just outside the closet. Reaching forward, he helped Kelsey to sit and then hoisted her by her shoulders to a standing position. Tugging at the tie he'd left knotted loosely around her neck, he led her out of the closet and turned her body so he could untie her wrists. Her hands were purple and he made a mental note not to tie her so tightly next time.

For there would be a next time. He found he was quite aroused by the sight of his girl bound in his neckties. Even if he had ruined them, it had definitely been worth it. It turned him on more than he'd expected to see her helpless and at his mercy.

He had always enjoyed bondage and BDSM porn sites, even if he'd never before dared to incorporate that kind of play in real life. But the rules were different now. There were no rules, except those *he* chose to make! The thought made his cock throb.

As the ties fell away, Kelsey's arms flopped down to her sides. James shoved the ties into his pocket and reached for her arms, rubbing them gently for a few moments. Bending down, he retrieved the handgun and waved it toward the small bathroom he'd had installed in the basement so he could wash up after his workouts.

"Go wash your face and use the toilet if you need to. Don't dawdle." Kelsey did as she was told, while James waited impatiently outside the open door.

When she was done, he again gestured with his gun, this time toward the gym equipment. "Go over there and lie down on your back on the weight bench," he ordered.

"But—"

"No." He cut her off. "No buts. Don't say a word. Do what I say. Do it *now*." James pointed the gun at her, and Kelsey did as she was told. She lay on her back, balancing herself with a leg on either side of the bench, feet flat on the ground. She wrapped her arms protectively over her torso.

"Don't move," James commanded, giving her a stern glare.

Keeping his eye on her, he moved quickly toward the work area. He opened the tool cabinet and rummaged until he found a neatly coiled hank of clothesline rope. Reaching for his work scissors, he returned quickly to Kelsey, who looked incredibly hot lying naked on his weight bench.

Sitting on the seat of the rowing machine, James rested the gun carefully in the water bottle holder. Kelsey was watching him with those lovely big green eyes as he cut several long pieces of rope. He stood and moved toward her.

"Please, James," she begged, hugging herself tighter. "Don't do this—"

"Kelsey," James interrupted firmly. "I said don't say a word, remember?" Bending down, he pressed two fingers over her pretty lips. "Don't make me hurt you."

She whimpered, tears springing to her eyes, but she gave a slight nod. Satisfied, James removed his hand. "Good. Now, I want you to reach up and grab the weight bar. Grip it nice and tight."

For several seconds Kelsey didn't move, her arms still clasped tightly over her breasts. Frowning, James reached for the gun. With a cry, Kelsey let go of her body and lifted her arms. She gripped the bar with shaking hands.

James wound and knotted the rope around her wrists, lashing her securely to the bar. He stepped back to admire his work. Christ, she was gorgeous! His eyes never leaving her, he pulled off his clothing and kicked it away. Kelsey was watching him, and he puffed out his chest and flexed his pecs and biceps. Surely she couldn't help but admire his muscles, which were well-defined and bulging, thanks to hours spent every week on this very equipment. Since Kelsey had joined the bank, he'd worked out extra hard every night while he bided his time for the exact correct moment to ask her out. Who would have dreamed he'd have her bound and naked in his basement, waiting for him to fuck her?

Unable to help herself, Kelsey's gaze traveled down to his cock, which was fully erect and bobbing toward her. She closed her eyes and turned her head away, but not before he saw the coldness in her face. This silent but blatant rejection wounded him to the core, and in spite of his promise to himself to go slow this time, rage spurred him into action.

"Bitch," he whispered furiously. He straddled her thighs, pinning her legs beneath him as he stroked his hard cock. He rubbed himself with his right hand and reached for her cunt with his left, pushing a finger inside her.

She wasn't wet. No matter. Pulling away his hand, he spit on his fingers and pushed inside her again, ignoring her squeal as he lubed her up. He made a mental note to bring some lubricant down to the basement for when he wanted to fuck her down here in the future. He would keep lube in every room until he taught her to love him. Then she wouldn't need any lube. She would be naturally wet.

He positioned himself between her legs and pressed the head of his throbbing cock against the entrance of her cunt. "God," he groaned. "I want you so fucking bad, Kelsey. So fucking bad."

As he pressed into her, she began to whimper.

"Damn it," he roared. "Don't cry!" Not that her crying would have stopped him. He couldn't have stopped if he tried. He was beyond caring about anything as her hot, tight, perfect cunt gripped his shaft, sucking him deep inside.

He leaned forward, gripping the bar on either side of her bound wrists for balance as he pummeled her cunt. Her breasts jiggled with each thrust and he let go of the bar with one hand so he could squeeze one perfect breast. He kneaded the flesh as he fucked her and then tugged at the nipple, twisting it until she squealed.

Christ. This was better than any fantasy. It felt so fucking good. So perfect. So right! There would be time later to make slow, extended, delicious love to his girl, but right now, in this moment, all he wanted to do was come. With a final slam, he released his seed deep inside Kelsey. The world was obliterated in a blinding explosion of pure, white heat, and then he collapsed against her, his heart smashing against his breastbone, sweat beading on his brow.

"Kelsey," he gasped into her ear. "Darling Kelsey. I love you."

~*~

He loves me? How *dare* he use that word for what he was doing to her?

James' weight was heavy on her, his sweaty body pinning her down, his cock still deep inside her. The shock and terror of what he had done to her was bad enough, but to cloak it with the pretense of *love?*

Turn it to your advantage. The voice was quiet but persistent in her head, penetrating the rank fear that skittered through her mind like a hoard of rats. *You know it's obsession, not love, but maybe he really believes his own lies. Play off that. Use it to get yourself out of this nightmare.*

Kelsey's eyes swiveled toward the gun. She clenched and unclenched her hands, trying to twist against the rope that was tight around her wrists. *I have to get that gun. I have to get hold of that fucking gun!*

She realized she was shaking beneath the deadweight of James' body. *Get off me!* she wanted to scream. *Get your disgusting, sweaty body off me, you fucking bastard!*

No. Stick to the plan. Lull him into complacency. Get the gun. That's all that matters.

"James?" she said softly, working to keep her voice low and soothing. "Can I get up now, please? It's hard to breathe with such a strong man on top of me."

James lifted himself on his arms and stared down at her, a small smile curling his lips. "I'm sorry, sweetheart. I guess I don't realize my own strength sometimes." To her relief, he rose from the bench. Kelsey closed her eyes to avoid looking at his naked body and glistening cock while he untied the ropes from around her wrists.

She brought her arms over her breasts and hugged herself as she watched him pull on his underwear and pants. Was this her chance? Did she dare roll from the bench and sprint for the gun? Even as the thought formed in her head, James, still shirtless, reached for the gun and tucked it into his pants pocket.

Okay, so she missed that chance. There would be others. She had no intention of meekly submitting to this deluded maniac for a second longer than she had to. Meanwhile, she just needed to play along. Just a little longer.

James held out his hand. Swallowing her revulsion, Kelsey forced herself to accept it, letting him pull her upright.

"I need a shower," James informed her. "You can shower with me. I'll let you soap up my cock and balls. Would you like that, Kelsey?"

Kelsey blinked. *Seriously?*

Play the game. He's nuts. Go along.

"Yes, James," she lied. "That sounds really hot."

Chapter 5

The hot water felt good spraying down over her body. If only she had been alone in her own apartment, she would shower for hours, scrubbing away every hint of James' defiling touch. Averting her eyes to avoid looking at James' hairy, muscular body in front of hers, Kelsey reached for the bar of soap.

James stopped her, placing his hand firmly over hers. "I'll do that. I'll wash your body and then you can wash mine."

Gee, thanks.

"Put your hands on top of your head," James ordered. He gripped her wrists, guiding her arms into position with strong hands. Kelsey had no choice but to obey. She closed her eyes, trying not to let her face show the rage and disgust she felt as James ran unwelcome hands over her breasts, under her arms and down her stomach.

He crouched in front of her in the large shower stall. "Spread your legs so I can wash your pussy and ass." Kelsey tried not to shudder as his fingers invaded her body. He scrubbed between her legs with soapy fingers. He rubbed for a long time over and around her labia, one finger worrying at her clit. If he was trying to arouse her, it definitely wasn't working.

Maybe this was her chance. She would jerk her knee upward, smashing it under his chin and knocking him backward so she could make her break. Before she could act, James stood and reached for her arms, which he forced around his body as he held her in a tight embrace.

"I'll teach you, darling," he murmured against her ear. "I'll teach you how to be more sexually responsive."

She wanted to spit in his face.

Finally he let go of her and stepped back. "I'll wash your hair. Sorry I don't have the right shampoo for you yet. I know you like those floral ones." He squirted shampoo into his hand and rubbed it on her head. "When I go to your place later, I'll get your shampoo and other stuff you need." He worked her hair into a lather as Kelsey absorbed this pronouncement. The thought of James slithering around in her apartment made her shudder.

"You cold, sweetheart? Here, let me make the water hotter." James adjusted the faucet and continued lathering her hair. His calling her sweetheart was like fingernails screeching down a chalkboard. How *dare* he call her that?

The gun. The gun. The gun. Kelsey's eyes slid to the door of the shower stall. Through the steamed glass she could just make out the weapon resting on the counter.

"Turn around and rinse your hair," James said, stepping back a little. "Then you can do me."

Kelsey rinsed her hair, taking as long as she dared, jittery with dreaded anticipation of what she knew James expected of her. Finally James grabbed her wrists with an impatient gesture. "Okay. Good enough. Here." He held out the bar of soap. "Soap up my cock and balls. I want you to give me a hand job. God, Kelsey. You have no idea—" his voice cracked. "I've imagined us together like this a thousand times. I can't believe it's finally real." He pressed on her shoulders. "Go on. Get on your knees. And look up at my face while you do it. Lick your lips while you stare up at me. Show me you like what you're doing."

Kelsey swallowed her outrage and forced herself to kneel in front of her captor. This was her chance. Get him going, get him distracted and then she'd make her move. Trying to hide her revulsion, she reached for James' sizable cock with one hand and cupped his heavy balls with the other.

His semi-erect shaft hardened immediately, distending like a clown balloon at her touch. She looked up at his face, trying to appear as if she enjoyed what she was doing. His eyes burning into hers, James groaned, "Yeah, baby. Kelsey. Kelsey, darling, yes!"

He reached for her shoulders to steady himself as she jerked at his hard, thick shaft, while cradling his balls with her other hand. He was panting. His eyelids fluttered closed, his head falling back.

Now! Do it now!

Her heart racing, Kelsey rocked over into the stall door, pushing it open with her shoulder. Dropping the man's genitals, she rolled out of the shower stall and scrambled to her feet. She hurtled toward the counter, her hand extended. She wrapped her fingers around the small, heavy weapon and whirled to face James. Triumph soared through her as she pointed the gun at him with shaking hands.

"What the hell!" the naked man roared, his eyes now wide open. He lunged out of the shower toward her.

Kelsey jumped back. "Don't move, asshole!" she screamed. "I'll shoot you! I'll fucking shoot you!" Her voice was shaking as much as her hands. She curled her trembling finger around the trigger, keeping the gun pointed in his direction. Water was dripping from her hair into her face and she shook her head, trying to see.

James halted just outside the shower stall. "Kelsey. Put that thing down. It's loaded. You'll hurt yourself." He started to walk toward her.

"I said don't move!" Kelsey blew out a breath and aimed the gun directly at James' heart, desperately trying to gird herself for what she knew she had to do. Her hands were shaking so hard she could barely keep hold of the gun.

She lowered the gun slightly. If he made a move, any move, she'd shoot him. Slowly, her eyes fixed on him, Kelsey began to edge backward toward the door. Just a few more seconds and —

"No!" James shouted. In spite of the gun pointing at him, he lunged toward her. Before she could react, he was on her. They fell to the floor, their wet bodies skidding slickly along the tile as they grappled. Kelsey heard herself wailing with fear and fury, and James' answering grunts as he tried to wrest the gun from her.

Kelsey pushed desperately against James, somehow managing to keep hold of the gun. She tried to pull her legs up to kick him away, but he was too strong for her. She felt his hands closing around her throat. This couldn't be happening. She had to shoot him. She had to do it! She had no choice.

She squeezed the trigger.

A sharp, deafening crack split the air and James fell away from her. In the sudden stillness that followed, a red hot burning pain ripped through Kelsey's leg. Time seemed to slip from its moorings, dragging Kelsey along with it.

Stunned and confused, she somehow managed to pull herself up on her elbows, the gun still dangling from her right hand. James was staring at her, his eyes wide with horror. His lips were moving but she couldn't hear any sound, save for the echo of the gun's report ringing in her ears.

James wasn't dead. He didn't even appear hurt.

Still not grasping what was happening, Kelsey followed his horrified gaze toward her leg, which throbbed with stinging pain. Bright red blood was pooling beneath her calf on the white tile floor. The room began to spin as a loud, rushing sound filled her head. She felt the back of her head hitting the floor and then she knew no more.

~*~

"Holy fuck. Holy shit," James cried. The sound of the gunshot still rang in his ears. "Kelsey. My darling, my baby…" Shaking, he crouched beside Kelsey. Her face was white as death. But she was breathing, he saw to his relief. It was just her leg. He let out a long, tremulous sigh of relief.

As he stared at the wound, James' training in emergency medicine from his brief stint as a volunteer firefighter kicked into gear. He checked her pulse, which was steady and strong. Though there was a lot of blood, it appeared the bullet had only grazed the skin rather than penetrating the muscle. She had probably just passed out from the shock.

He applied direct pressure until the bleeding slowed. Grabbing a towel, he ripped it into strips and tied a makeshift tourniquet around her leg. As he worked, he kept glancing at Kelsey's face. She would probably come to in a few seconds.

As he was working, the realization that someone might have heard the shot gave him pause. Though his neighbors kept pretty much to themselves, would the sound of a gun firing spur someone into calling 9-1-1?

Don't panic. They're probably all at work. And if anyone does question you, you have no idea what they're talking about.

James put the thought firmly from his mind. He had a patient to tend. He got a stack of towels from the linen closet. He used one to mop up the puddle of blood from the floor tiles, and slid the rest of them beneath her leg to elevate it. He pushed the wet strands of hair from her face and leaned close to her ear.

Gently, he shook her shoulder. "Kelsey. Kelsey, honey. Open your eyes. Everything's okay. You shot your leg, but it's just a flesh wound."

She moaned as he lifted her head and placed a folded towel beneath it. Her eyelids fluttered but didn't open. "Stay calm, stay calm," James murmured, not sure if he was talking to Kelsey or himself. He threw a washcloth in the sink and ran water over it, squirting some liquid soap on it as well. He retrieved the first aid kit from the cabinet and returned to Kelsey's side. Crouching again beside her, he carefully unwrapped the makeshift tourniquet from her leg.

The bleeding had stopped, which was an excellent sign that the damage wasn't too severe. He carefully blotted the torn flesh with the damp cloth and applied a thin layer of antibiotic cream. Finally he wrapped a thick padding of gauze and bandages around her calf to hold the wound closed while it healed.

As he worked, James was surprised to realize any vestige of the rage he'd experienced the night before due to her callous rejection had evaporated. He would be bigger than that, he told himself. Kelsey needed him. He would nurse his darling girl back to health. In the process she would come to understand how much he loved her, and she would be grateful for his care and devotion. From there, it would only be a short journey to love — he was sure of it.

Just as he finished applying the bandages, Kelsey came to with a sudden cry. Her eyes fixed blankly on his face and then she winced with pain. "What happened? Oh my god! You shot me! You shot me!" She began to wail.

"Shh, Kelsey, hush, it's okay. You're okay. I'm taking care of you."

Kelsey tried to twist away from him. Maneuvering himself so he was sitting behind her on the floor, James hoisted her upper body so she was leaning against his chest, and wrapped his arms tightly around her. He nuzzled her damp hair. "See what happens when you're a bad girl? You could have killed one of us. Luckily the bullet just grazed your leg." He kissed the side of her neck. "Now you need to calm down. You don't want to make it start bleeding again, do you?"

Eventually Kelsey stilled in his embrace, her wails quieting to a steady whimper. James cradled her in his arms, a sense of deep well-being pervading him. He kissed her neck tenderly and nuzzled her shoulder. Her bare breasts were perfect, her skin was so soft. He held her tight.

"I want to get you into the bed, Kelsey. I'm going to carry you, okay? I'm not going to hurt you. I'm just going to lift you into my arms and carry you into the bedroom. Don't try anything stupid, okay? Promise?"

She nodded and he released his tight hold of her. Standing, he bent over her and lifted the lovely, naked girl into his arms, careful not to jar her wounded leg as he carried her into the bedroom.

He laid her carefully on the bed. She was trembling, though from cold or shock he wasn't sure. He would have liked to stare for hours at her gorgeous body, but he reached for the covers and pulled them over her. When he reached down to stroke her cheek, she closed her eyes and turned her head away.

Poor darling, she was overwrought.

James stretched out beside her on the bed. Kelsey turned back toward him, her expression beseeching. "You can't keep this up. You can't keep me here. Jesus, James, this has gone way too far. Surely you can see that. Please, please, just let me go."

Her voice had risen to a hysterical pitch. She tried to fling the covers from her body. She pushed ineffectually at James, and when that didn't work, she tried to scoot down to the end of the bed. Alarmed she was going to hurt herself, James reached for her, catching her in a tight bear hug as he forced her head down to his chest.

"Kelsey, Kelsey, you need to calm down," he urged, as he pinned down her arms against his body. "You need time to rest and recover. You have to lie still."

Finally he let go of her. He pressed her gently but firmly against the mattress, making sure her head was comfortably resting on the pillows. "You're being a bad girl again, Kelsey." He smiled to take the sting out of his words and kissed the top of her head. "If you struggle like that again, I'll have to tie you down."

The image of her from the night before, wrists and ankles tied to the bed, legs spread wide, hair wild around her face, leaped into his mind and shot directly to his cock, which stiffened with the memory. He would have to be careful until her wound healed over a bit, but that didn't mean he couldn't have fun while nursing her back to health.

He could make it part of her training on how to be a good girl. He would tie her down and put her through a series of erotic exercises designed both to teach her and to please him. She would be punished or rewarded based on how quickly she learned to honor and obey the man who had chosen her.

The prospect excited him and he reached for his cock, giving it a hard pull. He wanted to fuck her then and there. He could almost feel the hot, wet tug of her cunt drawing him inside her, hugging his shaft in its tight embrace. It took every ounce of self-control not to lift himself over her and plunge into her.

The realization that she was crying dampened his lust. He was being selfish. He forced himself to focus on Kelsey's needs. "I'm going to give you some painkillers so you can sleep, okay?" She didn't respond. James let it pass. "While you're resting, I'm going to go over to your apartment and get some of your things. I know a girl likes to have her own things around her—makeup, shampoo, special nightie and whatnot. It only takes about ten minutes to get from my place to yours. I know a back route that avoids any traffic."

Her face was turned toward the wall, but at least she had stopped crying. He patted her thigh and stood. "I'll be right back." He loped to the bathroom and opened his medicine cabinet, glad he still had some of the pain medication left over from his knee surgery. It was powerful stuff.

He returned to the bedroom with a cup of water and two of the pills. "Here you go. Take these. They'll help with the pain." He pressed the small pills against her lips. At first she wouldn't open, but then a spasm of pain moved over her face, and her lips parted. James placed the pills on her tongue and held the small paper cup to her mouth. Kelsey drank.

"Will you let me go, James? Please?" She touched his arm.

He shook his head. She still didn't get it. "Rest, sweetheart. We'll talk when you wake up." She sighed, but she closed her eyes, again turning her head toward the wall. James sat quietly beside her, resisting the urge to stroke her hair, to cup her breast, to pull her close. Now was the time to be selfless. Later he would indulge his sensual desires. He would teach her to lust after him as he lusted after her. He forced himself to be contented with just looking at her, and marveling at the fact that he possessed her, and the realization they would be together forever.

Eventually her breathing slowed and deepened. "Kelsey," James said softly. She didn't respond. He touched her shoulder. She didn't move or react. James lifted himself carefully from the bed and went to the closet, retrieving the ties he'd used the night before, the ones he'd already designated in his mind as Kelsey's ties.

Reaching for Kelsey's left arm, he carefully looped the tie around her wrist and then lifted her arm over her head, bringing it to rest on the pillow. She didn't move. The dose of medicine he'd given her had knocked him out cold, and he was easily seventy-five pounds heavier than she was. She would probably be out for a while, which was all to the good. She needed her rest after the ordeal with the gun.

James quickly and quietly wrapped the second wrist and then tied them together and knotted the ends of the tie to the headboard, just in case she did wake while he was gone and get any crazy ideas about escaping.

He went into the bathroom and turned on the shower. While the water was heating, he mopped up the blood with the already-soiled bath towels and then piled the lot of them into a corner for later washing. He found the bullet and its casing and placed them carefully in the trash for later disposal. Finally, he retrieved the gun from the floor where it had fallen placed it carefully on the counter.

After a quick shower, James returned to the bedroom. He put the gun on the bureau, next to his wallet. He watched Kelsey sleep as he pulled on jeans and a polo shirt.

Naturally he knew where she lived. He couldn't even count the times he'd sat in his car in her apartment complex parking lot, watching to see when she might come out, and who was with her. Now he was going to see inside the place! He would touch her things and examine her possessions. He would select the items he would instinctively know she wanted. She would be grateful and happy to have her things around her. It would help her acclimate more quickly to the situation.

Moving toward the bed, he bent down and gently kissed the sleeping girl's forehead. "I'll be back soon, darling," he whispered.

Chapter 6

"I got your favorite. Here, have a sip."

Groggily, Kelsey opened her eyes. Something was pushing at her lips and she realized it was a straw. James was sitting on the bed beside her, holding a bottle of sparkling apple cider that was in fact her favorite thing to drink, and which she hadn't been able to find since she'd moved to the area.

"How did you —" she started to ask, but then bit her lip. She didn't want to know. She sipped at the bubbly drink as he held the bottle for her, avoiding his intense gaze. The dull throbbing in her calf bloomed into sharp pain as she came fully awake, and the traumatic and bizarre events of the last twenty-four hours unfolded in her mind like a horror movie. The straw fell from her lips as she gave a small cry.

"What? What is it, Kelsey? Are you in pain?" James set the bottle on the night table and reached toward her face. Instinctively Kelsey raised her hands to ward him off and saw the neckties dangling from her wrists. What the hell? Had he tied her to the bed while she'd been sleeping?

James smiled, his eyes glinting as he answered her unspoken question. "Just a precaution while I was gone," he said. "You looked super hot tied down like that. Did you ever engage in bondage play with Adam?"

His words hit her like a smack in the face, though she shouldn't have been surprised. She didn't reply. Seemingly unperturbed, James said, "Want to see the pictures?" He held up his cell phone, his tongue moving over his top lip like a cat licking its cream.

Kelsey shook her head, sliding her eyes away from the cell phone. She reached for the knotted silk on either wrist, fumbling to untie it. James slapped at her hands. "Stop that. I didn't tell you to take those off." He picked up a prescription bottle from the night table and shook a pill into his palm. "Take this. Just one this time, so you don't crash again."

He touched her lips with the pill and Kelsey opened her mouth, accepting it. When he placed the straw at her lips she reached for the bottle, but he pulled it away. "No, no. I'll do it." He held the straw again to her mouth and Kelsey sipped, hating him.

"When can I go home?" she said, trying to keep her voice calm and rational, as if that might somehow rub off on him. Surely he couldn't keep her there much longer. The whole thing was nuts.

"This is your home now, Kelsey. We can never go back to what was before. I'm sorry I took you by force, darling, but now that it's done…" He shrugged, letting the words hang.

Panic rose like bile in Kelsey's throat. "Listen to me, James," she said earnestly. She grabbed at the sheets to cover herself and tried to pull herself more upright. A white hot poker of pain shot through her calf. She winced and blew out a breath, but pushed on. "You can't do this. Just let me go. I promise I won't report you. I swear to god. I'll resign from the bank and—"

"Not necessary," James interrupted. "You already quit."

"What? I—"

"All taken care of," James rolled over her words with his. "I gave Reynolds the news early this morning. He was a little disappointed that you left so abruptly, but young people today..." Again James shrugged, adding a grin. The grin fell away as he reached for the sheet, ripping it away from Kelsey's naked body. "No one will miss you, Kelsey. You're mine now, don't you see? All mine."

The blood in Kelsey's veins turned to ice. "No!" she shouted. She shoved as hard as she could at James' chest and tried to swing her legs around him with a vague idea of leaping from the bed. The burst of blinding pain in her calf reminded her of just how disabled she was at the moment. Even if she managed to get up, how could she possibly hope to get away? A wave of dizziness made her sway, the walls swimming before her eyes.

James was like a rock against her efforts to shove him aside. Languidly he stood and reached for her wrists, catching both in one hand. He jerked her arms over her head and tied the neckties to the headboard, ignoring her struggles. "You're not behaving, Kelsey," he said with a shake of his head as he stared down at her. "And after all I've done for you."

"All you've done for me? What the fuck…?" Fury rendered her speechless, reddening her face and making her heart pound. She jerked hard against her restraints.

James nodded calmly. "Yes, all I've done for you. You don't know it yet, but you've found the love of your life." Kelsey gritted her teeth, rattling the headboard in her impotent rage. "I went to your apartment while you were resting. I watered your plants and collected your mail. I brought back some things I thought you might need."

He turned from her and bent down, pulling what she recognized as her red duffel bag from the floor. He set it on the bed and unzipped it. Reaching inside, he pulled out a round, flat plastic case she realized was her birth control pills. "You better take today's dose," he said, pushing a pill through the foil. "As much as I'd love to make a baby with you, we aren't ready yet to start our family."

The man was certifiably insane. Kelsey shuddered at the thought of having his child. She opened her mouth as he held out the small pill. He placed it on her tongue and she swallowed. Apparently satisfied, James settled next to her and began to pull things from the bag, placing them on the bed at her feet. He brought out bras and panties, clothing from her bureau and closet, several pairs of shoes and sandals, her makeup bag, blow dryer and her jewelry box.

"Now *this* looks like fun." James lifted of his eyebrows as he reached again into her bag. He regarded her with a sly smile as he held up the vibrator she kept in her night table drawer. Embarrassment and fury rose in equal proportions, heating her face and neck. If looks could have killed, James would have collapsed in a lifeless heap on the floor.

"No need to blush, sweetheart." James licked his lips again in what Kelsey assumed was supposed to be a sexy manner. "We're both adults. I like it that you, uh, pleasure yourself when you're alone. But that's all over now, my darling. Now I'll be the one to pleasure you. In fact"—his face brightened—"I think a good orgasm is probably just what you need right now. And if you please me, I'll let you up to use the bathroom, and I'll bring you something to eat and drink." He waved the purple phallus toward her. "But first, some fun."

"No, James," Kelsey blurted desperately. "Listen to me, damn it! I refuse—" James' hand was suddenly on her neck. He squeezed, his fingers tight just beneath her jaw and Kelsey's words strangled in her throat.

His voice was like a whip, each word a stroke. "You will not refuse anything I choose to give you, Kelsey. You belong to me now. The sooner you get that through your pretty but thick head, the better." He squeezed harder and Kelsey began to cough and choke. Tears sprang to her eyes as viselike pressure built behind her face. Oh god, was she going to die like this, naked and tied down in this madman's bed?

James let go abruptly and Kelsey sucked in a gasping breath of air. He stared down at her, his eyes glittering. "Don't make me hurt you, Kelsey. I want you to be a good girl, but if you continue to be bad, you'll leave me no choice but to punish you." He continued to stare at her with a hard, impenetrable gaze for several more long seconds. Kelsey stared back, speechless.

Finally James set the phallus upright on the night table and stood. He swept the rest of her things back into the duffel bag and dropped it on the floor next to the bed. He moved toward his closet, returning a moment later with a spare pillow, which he forced beneath Kelsey's ass.

"Spread your legs wide," he instructed. "Careful with the bullet wound," he added unnecessarily.

When Kelsey didn't react at once, he reached again for her throat. She spread her legs quickly, relieved when he dropped his hand. The pillow forced her hips and pelvis upward, as no doubt was his intention. James stood at the end of the bed, his eyes glued to her body as he pulled off his clothing. His cock sprang toward her, fully erect. Kelsey clutched her hands into fists above the ties, her body tensing with fearful anticipation.

He positioned himself between her spread legs and brought his face so close to her pussy she could feel his hot breath against it. Instinctively she tried to close her legs but he stopped her with a hand on either thigh.

Lowering his face, he touched her sex with the tip of his tongue. "Kelsey," he breathed. "You're so beautiful." He licked at her folds, moving his tongue in a circle around her clit. Kelsey tensed beneath his touch, trying again to close her legs as she jerked at the wrist restraints.

"Don't fight me, baby," James crooned. "I just want to make you feel good. Give in to it." Again he dipped his head and licked along the length of her pussy, his fingers digging into her thighs. Kelsey closed her eyes, trying to drift away in her mind, but it didn't work.

Finally he lifted his head. She could feel his gaze on her face, but she kept her eyes closed. She felt the lift of the mattress, and then the give as he sat beside her. She turned and opened her eyes to see what he was doing.

James was reaching again into the duffel bag. This time he pulled out her tube of personal lubricant. He reached for the vibrator and squirted the clear gel over its shiny rubber head. Scooting again between her legs, he touched the gooey head of the vibrator to her entrance and began to press it inside her. Kelsey tensed against the invasion, but he was persistent, pushing it until she was filled with the hard rubber phallus. He switched it on and it began pulse inside her with a steady hum.

"Christ, you look so fucking hot like that, Kelsey. You have no idea." James lifted himself from the bed and reached for his discarded jeans. Pulling his cell phone from a pocket, he aimed it in her direction and snapped several pictures. Setting the phone on the night table, he resumed his position between her legs.

James licked two fingertips and placed them against her clit. His touch was surprisingly light, his fingers moving delicately in a perfect counterpoint to the vibrator thrumming away inside her. In spite of herself, in spite of the fear, the pain in her leg, and her exhaustion, Kelsey felt herself succumbing to the barrage of stimulation. It was easier to give in than to fight, and she surrendered to the sensations.

"That's it, baby. Oh, yeah. Do it. Do it for me," James urged, his fingers moving in a flurry over her throbbing clit.

Kelsey tried to shut out his voice. She tried to forget that her hands were bound to the headboard, or that she was held captive in a madman's clutches. She focused on the pleasure radiating from her groin and let a moan pass her lips as the tremor of a climax spiraled out from her core. She felt the vibrator's speed and pulsation intensify and James began to move it in and out of her in a thrusting motion. In spite of her hatred of the man doing this to her, another climax moved through her body, this one more powerful than the last.

He kept at it, never giving her a moment to recover. "Enough," she finally moaned. "Please." She tried to close her legs, but the way James was positioned between them made it impossible.

"More," James insisted. "Give me everything you've got. I want it all."

On and on it went, James' fingers coupled with the pulsing phallus inside her pulling orgasm after orgasm from her exhausted body until Kelsey, sweating and panting, began to tremble uncontrollably.

"Please," she managed to gasp, "too much. It's too much. No more." Her moans edged up into a wail and she felt like she was going to pass out.

Finally, finally, he relented, withdrawing his fingers. He flicked off the vibrator and pulled it from her soaked cunt, though she continued to feel the echo of its pulse inside her.

James moved to sit beside her, his cock erect along his thigh. He reached for the cider bottle and held the straw to her lips. Kelsey drank gratefully and realized she was starving. James let her finish the cider and then set the bottle down.

"Please untie me, James," she begged. "I need to use the bathroom and I'm really hungry. My leg hurts."

"Soon," James said. "First there's this to take care of." He lifted himself over her and straddled her chest, gripping his large, fully erect cock and pointing it at her mouth. The head was purple, a drop of pre-come hanging from the tip.

"Open wide," he ordered, leaning forward as he guided his shaft toward her face.

Kelsey turned her head aside, pressing her lips together. She could taste the bile at the back of her throat.

"Hey!" James shouted. "You got yours. Now I get mine. Don't make me hurt you, Kelsey. Do what I say."

He gripped her jaw with hard fingers. "Open your mouth. Do it, girl." His voice was hoarse as he tugged at his cock, his stroke hard and quick. His body was heavy on her ribs, his balls settling between her breasts as he jerked at his shaft.

With a sudden movement, he reached out and slapped her across the face. When Kelsey gasped in pain and surprise, he shoved his penis into her mouth, pushing it deep until she gagged.

"Yeah," he moaned, "that's what I'm talking about." He began to thrust, each time going deep and making her choke. His balls hit her chin with each stroke, his thick, hard member filling her mouth.

At that moment Kelsey actually welcomed the throb of pain in her calf. She focused on it, letting it distract her from what was happening. This couldn't go on forever. He had to come soon. *Please, come. Come, come, come, you fucking asshole, you bastard, you prick.*

He gripped her face in his hands as he shuddered against her. Spurts of warm ejaculate filled her mouth, his shaft still resting against her tongue. She started to choke and, mercifully, the bastard pulled out. Kelsey turned her head and spit the salty goo onto the sheets.

"Hey, what the hell?" James grabbed her face again, forcing her to look at him. He was frowning, his brows furrowed. "You don't spit out my seed! You swallow every drop and then you thank me for coming in your mouth."

The edge of steel had returned to his voice. This see-sawing switch between creepy Mr. Lovey-dovey and Maniacal Abusive Man was worse than if he was just one or the other. Without knowing she was going to do it, Kelsey burst into tears. "Get off me! Let me go! Let me go! Let me go!" she yelled, choking on her tears as she cried.

He metamorphosed again, his face softening, his voice suddenly gentle. "Sweetheart, don't cry. I'm sorry. You're overwrought. I shouldn't have pushed you so fast, what with the bullet wound." Finally he climbed off her.

"My arms," she pleaded. "Untie me from the headboard."

He did, though the neckties remained tightly knotted at her wrists and he made no effort to undo them. Kelsey began to pick at them and he didn't stop her. Instead he held out another pill. "Take this. You need to rest some more," he said, still in lovey-dovey mode.

She let him put the pill on her tongue. There was no cider left, so she swallowed it without it. The salty, bitter taste of his jism coated her mouth. "I need to pee," she said. She managed to unknot the ties from her wrists and she flung them to the bed. "I need to brush my teeth. I haven't had anything to eat in hours."

James nodded. "I'll help you up. We'll walk together to the bathroom."

Having no choice in the matter, Kelsey allowed him to assist her to the bathroom. As she hobbled through the bedroom she glanced around the room, searching for the gun. If she got it again, she wouldn't hesitate to shoot him dead, but the gun was nowhere in sight.

As she sat on the toilet, she took surreptitious inventory of the bathroom, but saw nothing but the pile of bloody towels in the corner. *I have to get out of here. I have to get out. But how?*

James brought her toiletries into the bathroom and let her brush her teeth. Her hair had dried into a wild mess of wavy tangles and she tried half-heartedly to run her fingers through it but gave up. James, who was watching her, said, "I'll wash your hair later, darling. I brought your shampoo and conditioner."

A wave of woozy dizziness nearly overcame her as the pain pill took effect. James put his arm around her shoulders as he guided her back toward the bed. Kelsey let herself be supported as she limped back through the bedroom. She collapsed onto the bed and offered no struggle as James lifted and maneuvered her on the mattress. Her muscles had turned to rubber, her brain to mush. Food could come later. She just wanted to sleep.

James pulled the covers over her and bent down to kiss her forehead. Kelsey's eyelids were so heavy. She let them slide closed, welcoming the oblivion of drugged sleep with open arms.

~*~

James stared down at his lovely girl, wondering if he should tie her to the bed or not. It wasn't like she could get very far with that leg wound. Nor would she stir for a while with the drugs in her system. No, he would leave her be.

He moved to the bureau and pulled on a pair of clean underwear and some shorts. He was filled with a restless, wild energy that even the incredible blow job she'd given him hadn't dispelled. He couldn't wait to fuck her again.

First he had some work to do. He moved the gun to the top shelf in the hall closet. After another peek at his sleeping beauty, he returned to the kitchen, where he'd left the bag with his purchases from the sex boutique. Grabbing it, he hurried to the bedroom. He stood a moment just inside the door, drinking in the sight of Kelsey lying naked and sleeping in his bed. He moved into the room, tiptoeing toward the bed so as not to disturb her.

Kelsey didn't move a muscle, already deep into a drugged sleep. Her hair was a tousle of copper and red-gold against the pillow. Her eyelashes were so long they brushed her cheeks and there was a dusting of fine freckles on the bridge of her nose. Her lips were full and sensual, and his cock stirred with the memory of her hot mouth wrapped around it. They would have to do that again, and often.

While waiting for Kelsey to wake, James sat at his computer desk with the bag and took out the items one by one. He withdrew the hanks of rope and coils of chain. He wasn't entirely sure what he'd do with the chain, but the thought of it wound around Kelsey's neck, wrists and ankles had given him a boner in the boutique, so he'd bought it.

He pulled out a pair of leather wrist cuffs and a black suede flogger. It had cost a fortune, but James knew it would be worth it. The man behind the counter had assured James with a knowing leer that it packed a delicious sting while still getting its point across. James wasn't sure about the delicious part, at least not for the person on the receiving end, but that wasn't why he'd bought it.

As he'd been going through her apartment, and on the drive there and back, James had found himself deeply excited by the idea of "training" Kelsey to become his ideal woman. The thought of her misbehaving and having to be punished gave him an instant erection. The image of her naked and bound while he smacked her perfect little ass with the flogger…!

Jesus, just the image was so powerful he could practically come just picturing it.

It was wrong to raise your hand to a woman, ever, for any reason. He knew that. Of course he did. And yet, those rules applied to the real world, to the world of rules and prescribed, civilized behavior.

When he'd taken Kelsey last night with unbridled passion, he'd crossed the line, taking her along with him. They had left that so-called civilized world behind. There were no rules where they now resided, or rather, the rules were just waiting to be written — by him.

Chapter 7

"About time you woke up, sleepy head." James set the breakfast tray on the night table and sat beside Kelsey. He had been up for a while, but had wanted to let her get her rest. He had barely slept the night before, so enamored of having Kelsey in his bed, in his arms. He found he liked that better than having her tied down as she had been the night before. In some ways, her having shot herself was a blessing in disguise. He couldn't deny he loved the idea of having her physically dependent on him.

He'd given her another pain pill at about two, and she'd sunk back into a drugged sleep until morning. He only had a few of the pills left, but that was for the best. Now that the worst of her pain was probably past, he wanted her alert for all the delicious things he had planned for her.

"Let's see how your leg is doing." Carefully he removed the bandages, pleased to see the swelling had gone down, the skin already beginning to mend. He smiled at Kelsey. "It's looking better already. Another week or so and you should be able to get around on your own."

Kelsey didn't respond. James carefully cleaned and gently re-bandaged her leg. Kelsey was staring at the tray of food while he worked.

"Hungry?" James asked.

Kelsey swallowed and nodded, still not speaking. James lifted the tray and set it carefully on the bed beside her. "I sliced you a fresh peach," he offered. "There's oatmeal and some toast. Plus I made you a cup of coffee, just the way you like it."

Kelsey hoisted herself up on the pillows, wincing slightly. She reached for the mug of coffee. "No, no," James said, swatting her hand aside. "I'll feed you. I'm going to take total care of you. Your only job right now is to open your mouth, swallow and chew."

"But—"

"No buts," James said firmly. "I insist."

"I don't like oatmeal," she responded, a cute pout on her lips.

"Don't be silly. I added raisins and brown sugar—"

"I really *hate* oatmeal," she rudely insisted.

James glared at her, annoyed. He'd spent a lot of time making that oatmeal for her. Then he softened. The poor thing had so much to handle right now. And she didn't know the rules yet. He would teach her the rules, and then things would go better.

He offered a small shrug. "Okay. No oatmeal. You want the peach and toast?"

"Yes, please."

That was more like it. James speared a slice of peach with the fork and brought it to her lips. Kelsey took the fruit into her mouth, closing her eyes as she chewed.

"More?" James asked.

"Coffee, please," she said, and he obliged, holding the mug to her lips and carefully tilting the hot liquid into her mouth. She drank half the cup before settling back against the pillows. "James," she sighed. "I really can feed myself."

"I said no," James said firmly. "This isn't about what you can or can't do. It's about what I want. And I want to feed you. End of discussion."

Wow. It felt amazing to say that. When had anything ever been truly about what *he* wanted? Especially where women were concerned. Feeling expansive, he picked up the toast and held it toward her. "Want a bite?" he inquired solicitously.

Though her expression was mutinous, Caitlin nodded. He would soon wipe that insolence from her face, but for now he just held the toast to her mouth. Crumbs fell on her bare chest, and he wiped them away, making a mental note to bring one of his cloth napkins on the next meal tray.

When all the coffee, fruit and toast were gone, James dipped a spoon into the oatmeal. "How about just a bite?" *I could make her,* he thought, but decided against it. Just the knowledge that he had that power was enough—for now.

"No," Kelsey said forcefully, and then in a more contrite tone, "No, thank you. I'm — I'm full. Thanks. Can I use the toilet now?"

James removed the tray and balanced it on the night table. He stood and reached for Kelsey's arm, helping her out of the bed. She leaned heavily against him as they made their way to the bathroom. He let her use the toilet in relative privacy, leaving the door ajar as he stepped into the bedroom. When he heard the toilet flush, he returned and helped her to the sink, allowing her to brush her teeth and wash her face.

"I'll wash your hair later and give you a sponge bath," James said, regarding her in the mirror. "Come back to bed first. We have some important matters to discuss."

"James," she began, "this really can't go on. You're going to—"

James reached for her shoulders from behind and gripped them hard as he stared at her face in the mirror. "Kelsey, you need to stop. I've told you already, what's done is done. There is no going back. You and I are partners now. I know you don't love me yet, but I'm hopeful you'll come to have feelings for me, once you understand how much I adore you."

Kelsey's eyes met his in the mirror, a look of incredulity on her face. James felt a vein pulse in his temple and he clenched his teeth. Was it really such a stretch to think they might fall in love? He was head and shoulders above any of those idiots who had sniffed around her at the bank. She could certainly do worse than him for a life partner. He was reasonably good-looking and, though she didn't yet know it, quite wealthy. More importantly, he loved *her*. Didn't she get that?

James let go of her shoulders and took a step back. He forced himself to take a deep, cleansing breath, which he let out slowly. He would teach her. She'd learned quickly on the job—she would learn quickly at home. He would see to it. "Come on," he said, keeping his voice gentle. "Come back to bed."

Kelsey allowed herself to be led, James supporting her with a strong arm around her back, half-carrying her so she needn't put any weight on the wounded leg. He helped her back onto the mattress and pulled up his desk chair to the side of the bed so he could face her as they talked.

"So," he said, "I've been giving it a lot of thought, Kelsey. I think it's time we make some of your secret sex fantasies come true."

Kelsey wrinkled her cute little nose at this pronouncement, which made him smile. "I do love the thought of you making love with another woman while your lover, in this case, me, watches, but we're not ready yet to bring anyone else into our relationship."

Her mouth had fallen slightly open, and James smiled knowingly at her unasked question. "Then there's the fantasy about you being with two guys who are both really into you. You know you have to choose one of them by the end of the night, but meanwhile you just revel in all the erotic attention."

Her cheeks were suffusing with pink, her mouth opening wider into a pretty little O. "How do you…" she breathed, not finishing the question.

"I know a lot of things." James grinned. "I have to say, my favorite is your 'slave for a day' scenario, you know, the one where you submit to all your boyfriend's sexual desires, no matter how outrageous or out there they are." He rubbed his hands together. "That's one we can enact right away. I have a lot of ideas of my own in that regard, you can be assured."

Kelsey stared at him blankly for several seconds, and then he saw the light go on. "That's how you did it," she breathed, the color draining from her face. "You're Brittney."

James gave a modest nod, smiling. "At your service," he agreed. "It was an interesting experiment pretending to be a female. I have to say, I find the constant use of that annoying little initialism *LOL* quite tedious, but it seems to be what all the girls use, so…" He shrugged. "I had to do some research about your high school to seem credible." He shook his head, offering Kelsey an ironic smile. "You really should be more careful who you friend on Facebook,

Kelsey, and who you choose to share your secrets with. Don't you know there's no privacy on the internet? Once you put it out there, it's potentially available for the whole world to see."

"Wait, wait," Kelsey said, wrapping her arms around herself, her brows furrowing. "I *know* Brittney Davis. I mean, I knew her six years ago. She went to high school with me. She has a Facebook page and everything. You *can't* be Brittney. You can't!"

"She was three years behind you in school, right? When we first chatted, you admitted you didn't really remember her all that well."

"Jesus," Kelsey whispered.

"Pretty good, huh?" James said, pleased. "I spent a lot of time putting that Facebook page together. It was easier than I expected, actually. I downloaded pictures of likely candidates from your high school and went *phishing*. Isn't that what they call it? I put out a few other names as bait before you responded, but Brittney was the one that caught you and then it was just a matter of reeling you in. I, as Brittney of course, friended a bunch of other people from your high school to look more legit." He gave a small, satisfied chuckle. "I have to say, I really had no idea how easy it is to pose as someone else. Easily seventy-five percent of your high school classmates on Facebook accepted my friendship without hesitation or question. But *you're* the only one I talked to. You're the only one I wanted. The only one I ever wanted."

Kelsey fell back against the pillows and closed her eyes. James leaned down so he could kiss her pouty mouth. Kelsey twisted her head away and a clap of rage exploded inside him like a firecracker. "Damn it!" he shouted. "Don't you get it? This is way more than some office crush. This is about true love, Kelsey. The kind you've only dreamed of. Stop fighting me at every turn."

James realized his hands had curled into fists. Kelsey was staring at him as if he were a monster, instead of the man of her dreams. He pressed his lips together and blew out a long breath. He needed to calm down. This wasn't going the way he'd envisioned it.

Forcing himself to speak in a soothing voice, he continued, "Look, I know how lonely you've been since the breakup with Adam, even though we both know he wasn't right for you. But that's all over now. We have each other."

James felt his compassion returning, and he smiled gently at his true love. He could see the emotions moving over Kelsey's face like a storm. Had what he'd said finally penetrated that sweet, thick skull of hers? Or was she going to continue to deny what they shared. She clearly wanted to say something. He waited patiently.

"James," she finally said in an exasperated tone. "I get that you think you have strong feelings for me, but you don't even really know me. And with what's happened — with what you've done — "

"Enough!" The rage he'd managed to tamp down roared to life again. He stood abruptly and paced in a tight circle beside the bed. He whirled on the girl who kept throwing barbs directly into his heart. "I only told you about the Facebook thing because I wanted you to understand that I *do* know you, not just the persona you present at work, but the real Kelsey Anne Rowan. The girl who moved so often in her childhood because of her father's job that she was always 'the new girl' at school and never felt like she fit in. The girl who hates math, who always felt like an imposter in her business major but stuck with it because she knew she could earn a living that way. The girl who used to sing alto in the choir and who likes to paint. The girl who wants three children someday, and whose favorite color is green, and who has an older brother who's into drugs and hardly ever shows up for family holidays, except when he needs money. The girl who thinks her boss is kind of cute" — his smile edged into a grin — "if a little nerdy."

Kelsey was staring at him, making no effort to disguise her horror. He wasn't reaching her. If anything, he was pushing her away.

James sat heavily on the bed. He looked at the woman he loved and made a decision. "I'd planned to wait until your leg had healed a little more to introduce the concept of punishment, but I think the time has come. As I've learned as a team manager at the bank, some folks respond well to a soft approach. Others need their lessons beaten into them. I'm coming to think you fit into the latter category."

He jumped up, his resolve strengthening. He turned the chair so its back was perpendicular to the mattress, and reached for the naked girl, pulling her forward onto her stomach. "Ow!" Kelsey cried. "Let go!"

"Don't struggle. You'll hurt your leg." James hauled the upper half of her body over his lap, leaving her legs to stretch out on the mattress. Her breasts were pressed against his groin, her head hanging at his left hip. He was in complete control. She was at his mercy. His cock hardened.

"You're a very bad girl, Kelsey Anne," he informed her. "And bad girls have to be punished. You're going to get a good, hard spanking." Placing one hand firmly on her lower back, he brought his hand down hard on her pert little bottom. Kelsey squealed, trying unsuccessfully to pull away. He smacked her again, admiring the reddening imprint of his hand on her skin. He could feel power radiating from his fingertips and tingling in his palms.

He continued to smack her, alternating between cheeks until they were both hot to the touch and cherry red. She continued to squirm and squeal, but he didn't stop, a dark, wild force driving him on. His cock throbbed but he didn't stop. She needed to be taught a lesson, and he was the man to teach her.

He struck her ass over and over until his hand was stinging from the impact. The struggle had finally gone out of her, and she was whimpering. James eased off the spanking, now lightly stroking her flaming ass cheeks.

What would it be like to fuck her freshly spanked ass? He ached to find out then and there, but not with her wound still so fresh. No, he would be patient for the sake of his girl. Instead he pushed the chair back, carefully supporting Kelsey as he shifted the upper half of her body back onto the bed.

No, he wouldn't fuck her yet, but that didn't mean he wouldn't take his pleasure. Unable to resist a moment longer, James stood and yanked off his clothes. He fisted his pulsing cock and tugged at it with a groan.

Kelsey lay motionless on her stomach, her face hidden in a tangle of coppery tresses, her pretty bottom a lovely contrast in red to the white of her thighs and back. James stroked himself rapidly, the urgency of his need overwhelming him.

"Kelsey, Kelsey, my darling," he murmured breathlessly as he brought himself quickly to orgasm. She didn't move or respond, save for her steady, quiet whimpering. Within minutes he spurted ribbons of pearly-white ejaculate over her soundly-spanked ass. He touched the jism lightly with his fingers, swirling it in patterns over her hot, red ass cheeks. With a satisfied sigh, he sank onto the bed beside his girl. Glancing toward her leg, he saw that the wound had started to seep blood through the bandages.

Dismay nearly obscured the pleasure from his powerful orgasm. He reached toward her leg, lightly touching her wounded calf. "You silly girl," he admonished gently, "you've made yourself bleed."

~*~

James was snoring, a heavy arm thrown over Kelsey's midriff. "James," she whispered. No response. Carefully, oh so carefully, she began to inch away from beneath his arm, stopping in her progress every few seconds to make sure he was still sleeping soundly. Finally she managed to ease far enough from him that his arm flopped to the bed.

She held her breath.

He continued to snore.

Her leg didn't hurt quite as much as it had. The sharp, shooting pains had eased into a steady, dull throb. Her bottom still stung from the spanking. But beyond the pain and humiliation of the spanking was the shock that it was happening at all. The whole time he was smacking her with his hard palm, she could feel the insistent bulge of his cock beneath her body. He clearly got off on this "good girl/bad girl" thing he'd worked up in his mind. At least he'd only jerked off over her, though that had been horrid enough.

Afterward he'd carried her in his arms to the bathroom and placed her gently in the tub. He'd cleaned her wound and then washed her hair beneath the faucet with loving attention. He'd insisted on feeding her again, this time a grilled cheese sandwich and a mug of tomato soup. While it was annoying as hell to have someone else feeding her, he seemed really tender and happy while he was doing it. It was impossible to reconcile his brutal behavior with his loving, if bizarre, ministrations afterward. She honestly didn't know what to make of the man.

One thing she knew for sure—he was stark raving mad.

She glanced anxiously at James, who was still snoring softly, and then at the clock beside the bed. It was a little after three in the afternoon. She guessed he'd been asleep for nearly an hour. There was no telling when he'd wake from his little nap, or what dreadful things he had in store for her.

I have to get away. Get to a phone. Call 9-1-1.

This thought fueled her as she inched her way down the mattress. It seemed like hours, but she finally reached the bottom of the bed. Carefully she eased herself to the carpet, sinking to her knees. It was easier to crawl than to walk, and she moved as quietly as she could on her hands and knees, glancing back to the bed every few seconds.

She crawled to the pile of clothing he'd left in a heap on the floor, feeling frantically for his cell phone. It wasn't there.

Fuck.

She looked desperately around the bedroom, but there was no evidence of a landline. Where the hell was his cell? It wasn't on the bureau either. Not ready to give up, not by a long shot, she grabbed James' T-shirt and pulled it over her head. She continued her stealthy crawl, forcing herself to ignore the rising pain in her calf as she dragged that leg along. He'd left the bedroom door open a few inches. Kelsey reached for it, pushing it gently and then freezing as the hinges creaked, the sound squealing through the room like a wounded animal.

She whipped her head back toward the bed. James hadn't moved. Her heart was galloping in her chest.

Just get out the door.

The bedroom exited onto a short hallway. There was another room just across from it but Kelsey turned left, heading into the living room, thanking whatever gods there might be that James lived in a one-story house.

She pulled herself upright on the sofa and scanned the room, searching for a phone. No luck. She thought about how he'd brought her in through the kitchen. Maybe he put his phone and wallet down there when he'd come in earlier, or maybe, if he did have a landline, it was there.

Adrenaline and fear pushed her along as she hobbled and hopped toward the kitchen. She swept the room with her eyes. No phone. No wallet. No landline.

"Fuck," she whispered.

Just get out. Get out!

It had been dark, and she'd been in a state of hysterical panic by the time he'd pulled into the garage the night before. She hadn't noticed what kind of neighborhood he lived in, or if there were likely to be people outside. All she needed was to be seen. She would scream for help. And she would be rescued, and this horrible nightmare would be at an end.

She weighed her options. Did she head back through the living room to the front door, or go out the kitchen door, which presumably led to James' backyard? That door was much closer, and she decided to go that way. Supporting herself along the counters, she made it to the back door. She turned the deadbolt and opened the door.

The warmth of the summer day hit her with a blast of humidity, bringing with it the promise of freedom. Flinging the door wide, she hobbled outside, putting as little weight as she could on her bad leg as she hopped and limped down the three steps to the grass.

She glanced quickly around and cursed. The small backyard was walled in by a high wooden fence. She couldn't see into the neighbors' yards and they couldn't see her.

But they could hear her.

"Help!" she cried, her voice hoarse from disuse. She cleared her throat. "Help me!" she screamed as she hopped toward the gate as quickly as she could. "Help—"

All at once the wind was knocked out of her lungs and she fell heavily to the grass, momentarily stunned. She felt herself being hauled to her feet and then flung over a man's shoulder. His arm clamped hard around the back of her thighs and her head bumped against his bare back as James carried Kelsey back into the house.

He kicked the back door closed with his foot and set her, none too gently, on a kitchen chair. Her leg was screaming, her heart pounding, her head reeling. She had been so close. So close!

"No!" she heard herself wailing, as if from a remove. "No, no, no! You can't do this. Let me go! Let me—" She was stunned into silence by the back of his hand smashing against her mouth.

"You," James said, glaring at her, his eyes dark with fury, "are a very, *very* bad girl." It was only then that she saw the gun in his hand. He waved it in her direction. "What happens to bad girls, Kelsey? Tell me!"

Kelsey touched her face, which was stinging from the blow. Her lower lip was split and bleeding and she touched it gingerly with her tongue. She stared at James' angry face and then at the muzzle of his gun, speechless with terror.

This was it.

She was going to die.

The oxygen in the room vanished, leaving her gasping like a fish out of water, her heart pounding in a deep, steady boom. Her bones melted inside her body and she felt herself sliding from the chair to the floor, powerless to stop herself. The world shifted and cracked wide, and she welcomed the opening chasm, slipping soundlessly into the arms of the enveloping darkness.

Chapter 8

James didn't wait for her to regain consciousness. He scooped her into his arms and pushed open the door that led to the garage with his hip. He managed to get the car's passenger door open, and he slid her into the seat. Grabbing some bungee cords he kept on a shelf in the garage, he pulled her arms behind the seat and used the cords to bind them tight.

He knew already what must be done. He'd been a fool to think he could keep Kelsey at his house, at least not until she came to understand that her place was at his side. He had been an idiot to fall asleep without first tying her down. He had come *that* close to losing her. If he hadn't woken when he had, she might even now be jabbering to some policeman, painting the story of what had transpired between them in black and white, leaving out the rich, colorful tapestry of love beneath what might seem like brutal actions to the uninformed.

These thoughts crowded his mind as James flew through the house. Hurriedly he pulled on jeans, a T-shirt and a pair of sandals. He threw some of his clothing and toiletries into the duffel that contained the things he'd retrieved from her apartment. He would come back later for more clothing and supplies, once he had Kelsey properly settled in the cabin. He swept the sex toys still waiting on his computer desk into the bag as well, excited at the thought of using them all. Lastly he grabbed his laptop, placing that in the duffel as well.

He glanced at the pictures of his beloved that covered the walls. Those would have to come down, but there was no time now. He would return later in the week to remove any evidence of his secret obsession, just in case.

For the first time, he found himself glad that his parents were no longer living, and that his sister, with whom he'd never been close anyway, resided over a thousand miles away. He needed no one but Kelsey. And she needed no one but him. The family vacation cabin by the lake would be the perfect hideout while he trained her to adapt to her new life as his soulmate and most prized possession.

He slung the duffel over his shoulder and, gun in hand, raced back to the kitchen, where he locked the back door and set the alarm before returning to the garage. He could see Kelsey through the car widow. She had regained consciousness and was struggling mightily to get free of the bungee cords.

He pulled open the passenger door and aimed the gun in her direction. "Stop it!" he ordered tersely. "I don't have time for this shit right now, Kelsey." He saw that the gauze he'd wrapped over her bandaged wound was red with new blood, and a rush of guilt washed over him. But it was her fault. She shouldn't have run outside like that. He'd had no choice but to tackle her.

Ignoring her yelping demands to be let go, he leaned over the backseat to inspect how the bungee cords were holding up. She had nearly managed to wrench herself out of them; one hand was almost freed. James tossed the duffel on the backseat and placed the gun beside it. He adjusted the cords, winding them more tightly around her arms and giving them a tug to make sure she couldn't get out of them during the drive.

Once satisfied she wasn't going anywhere, James grabbed the gun and hurried around the car to the driver's seat. Setting the weapon just under his seat, he reached across Kelsey and pulled the seatbelt over her body. He buckled her in, positioning the belt so it rested between her luscious breasts. It was good she'd put on his T-shirt. He couldn't very well take her on the highway naked, though he would have liked to. She looked disheveled, her hair wild, a smudge of dirt on her cheek, but he doubted anyone driving by them would notice or care.

"James, where are we going? Where are you taking me?" Kelsey's normally low, sultry voice was pitched an unpleasant octave too high. "The cords are too tight," she whined. "My arms hurt. My leg hurts. You can't do this. Damn it, you bastard! You have to—"

Her squealing was making his head throb. Without thinking, James lifted his arm and smacked her mouth with the back of his hand. "Shut the fuck up, Kelsey. Just shut up."

She was staring at him with wide, frightened eyes. Her cheeks looked unnaturally pale, especially in contrast to the thin trickle of bright red blood that had appeared on her pouting lower lip.

"Damn it," he swore. "See what you made me do?"

She didn't answer. A single tear rolled down her cheek and James' anger melted away. "I'm sorry," he said. "I shouldn't have hit you in anger." He knew he needed to control his temper better. He needed to have patience until Kelsey learned her lessons properly. The sooner they got where they were going, the sooner the lessons could start.

As he backed the car out of the garage, he reached over to pat her thigh. She flinched, her body tensing, and he realized she thought he was going to strike her again. "Hey, relax. You need to stay calm and quiet while I'm driving, okay? Just relax." He pushed the button on the garage door remote and watched the garage door begin its descent before turning his attention to the road behind him in the rearview mirror.

He pulled smoothly onto the street and headed toward the highway. Though his foot itched to push the peddle to the metal and burn the tires in a screech of rubber, he forced himself to drive at a sedate pace. Once on the highway he would stick to the speed limit, and take no chances.

"I've decided this neighborhood isn't the proper place for us while we get to know each other better," he said, glancing at her with a smile. She didn't smile back.

A drop of the blood from her split lip had splashed onto her collarbone. Though he did feel bad for having lost his temper, James couldn't deny the rush of power, the erotic thrill that the sight of her blood caused deep inside him. His cock pulsed and twitched in his jeans. Christ, he wanted to fuck her then and there.

His voice came out hoarse with lust when he started to speak. He cleared his throat and started again. "I'm taking you to my cabin by the lake. I own quite a large plot of land there and the cabin is set a good two miles back from the road. It's nice and secluded, far from prying eyes and nosy neighbors."

She said nothing in reply, but at least she'd stopped her squawking. James turned his attention back to the road, each mile that passed taking them closer to their love nest. Once they were on the highway and enjoying a long stretch of travel with little traffic around them, James reached over to stroke Kelsey's bare thigh.

Kelsey's seat was pushed back to the perfect angle for the delicious idea that leaped suddenly into James' brain. Her skin was like warm silk and he let his fingers glide over it toward her cunt, which he knew was bare beneath the oversized T-shirt.

"No!" Kelsey dared to protest.

James gave her thigh a sharp slap. "Yes," he retorted. "Do you want to be punished? Keep it up, and that's what will happen."

She had started to whimper. "Kelsey," he said in a cajoling tone, "you don't get it yet, but I'm not the enemy. I'm the best thing that's ever happened to you, if you give it a chance. And I can give you pleasure, if you'll let me. I can make you come while I drive. Would you like that, baby? I know just how to touch you."

Still no response. He would teach her to answer when spoken to, and to answer with the proper respect. He slid his hand again over her leg, this time pushing his fingers between her thighs. He was pleased when she didn't resist him.

He cupped her mound. He had been thinking about whether he would shave her cunt, like all the girls in the porn videos. He rather liked the delicate sweep of soft, auburn curls that hid her pretty sex, but on the other hand, it would be hot to shave her. There was something supremely erotic about the thought of the cold, sharp razor scraping against the tender skin of her private parts, over and over until she was smooth.

His cock was uncomfortably bent in his jeans, and he pulled his hand away so he could adjust himself. He licked his fingers and reached again for the prize between her legs. "Spread your legs," he ordered. "I'm going to make you come while I drive. I've always wanted to do that."

She said nothing, which was much better than whining and squealing, and she obeyed, shifting on the leather seat as she opened her legs for him. He stroked the soft labia with his wet fingers, moving lightly over her clit in a teasing motion. His cock ached and he had to remind himself to focus on the road. But he didn't stop touching her.

He rubbed and stroked her sweet cunt, teasing her clit until he felt it stiffen beneath his fingers. He spent a long time, his touch light as feathers, but relentless nonetheless. After several minutes, he finally moved his fingers down, seeking her tight entrance. Her cunt was hot and moist as he slid his finger inside her.

He looked at Kelsey. She had closed her eyes. Her nipples jutted prettily beneath the T-shirt, the position of her bound arms forcing her breasts forward. Her lips were parted and there was a flush creeping up her neck.

Christ, she was sexy. She was so responsive. Even in the face of her fear, or maybe, he thought with an excited rush, partially because of it, she was aroused by his touch. He used his palm to grind against her clit as he fucked her tight, hot cunt with his fingers. She was panting, and all at once she stiffened. He could feel her cunt spasming against his fingers. James nearly came in his pants just watching the girl.

When he finally pulled away his hand, he brought it to his face and breathed in the delicate, erotic scent of her musk, which clung to his fingers like the finest perfume. He glanced again at his girl. She had turned her face toward the window. He decided to let her be. He knew he'd been taking a stupid risk, letting her distract him to such a degree while he was driving. He needed to focus on the road more so he could get them where they were going without incident or accident. He needed to take better care of his precious cargo.

He glanced again in her direction. Her face was still turned away, her head now resting against the back of the seat. The thought of how close he'd come to losing her earlier that day made him grip the steering wheel so tightly his knuckles turned white. He would be more careful going forward to make sure she didn't try to run away again.

You're mine now. I'll never, ever let you go.

~*~

Though it seemed impossible, Kelsey must have actually drifted to sleep, because she came awake with a jerk, taking a second to orient herself. James was humming softly beside her.

She'd been intending to pretend to come after a decent interval so he'd leave her alone, but had surprised herself by actually orgasming against his fingers. It was that thing he'd done with his palm, she realized. Whatever it was, it had worked, and once she had climaxed, he had, thank god, let her be.

He was watching the road, and she was glad of at least a moment without his unwelcome attention focused on her. Her mouth was dry, her arms numb, her leg aching. Her tongue worried the split on her lower lip from his repeatedly backhanding her. James had a temper, one he'd hidden remarkably well when at the office, but he'd hidden far more than that in the months they'd worked together.

Kelsey tried to bring her hands to her face to push away her hair, but the tight grip of the bungee cords around her wrists quickly reminded her that she could not. Warily she glanced again in his direction, glad he hadn't yet noticed she was awake. She stared at his profile. He had an aquiline nose and a square, masculine jaw. With his gray eyes, dark, straight hair and muscular build, he was an attractive man.

She remembered with sudden horror that she'd confided this to the person she'd *thought* was Brittney from high school, the "girl" who had so eagerly friended her on Facebook. She had shared with the false Brittney about her boss at the bank, admitting that she'd considered going out with him, even if he was kind of nerdy and quiet. She remembered how Brittney had said those quiet ones were the ones to watch out for. They were usually dynamite in bed, she'd said. Now that Kelsey thought about it, it was Brittney, a.k.a. James, who had brought up the subject of dating in the workplace.

And to think, she'd been sitting in that front desk all those months, under James' watchful eye. Christ, for all she knew, he'd been masturbating under his desk while he slyly watched her working. And all those pictures of her on his bedroom walls! From literally the moment she'd joined the bank, he'd begun to stealthily stalk her. Maybe he'd planned this whole thing all along. And now he was taking her somewhere secluded — somewhere no one would ever be able to find her.

The thought made her squeak with fear, the sound bursting from her lips before she could stop it. James turned in her direction and smiled. "There she is," he said in a jovial tone, as if everything were fine and dandy. "I was wondering when you'd wake up. We're almost there."

She realized they had left the highway and were now driving along a narrow road that was bordered on both sides by tall, swaying grasses and wildflowers, beyond which loomed a thicket of brush and trees. James slowed the car and turned onto an even narrower road. As the trees thinned, the view expanded to gently rolling hills and the shimmer of gold coins dappling a large lake in the setting sun.

Each bounce of the car along the rutted, unpaved lane sent a jolt of pain through Kelsey's hurt leg. She shifted on the seat, trying to get more comfortable in her awkward position. "My arms are asleep," she said, unable to keep the whine from her tone. "Can you please take these cords off? There could be permanent damage from lack of circulation."

James didn't look at her as he replied. "You'll be fine. We'll be at the cabin in a minute or so, and I'll untie you then." He glanced in her direction with a warning expression. "Do you promise to be a good girl from now on?"

What the fuck did that even *mean*? She wasn't eight years old, for god's sake, and he sure as hell wasn't her father. No, he was just a sick bastard, apparently determined to play out some kind of sado-masochistic Master/slave scenario. How did she fight, when he had all the power, and she had none?

You have to be more cunning than he is. Keep your wits about you. Bide your time. Your strongest weapon is his love, or what passes for love in his twisted psyche. Use it, Kelsey.

She would take her fight underground. She would let James think the violent, sociopathic obsession he called "love" was being reciprocated. She would have to be careful though. Whatever else he was, James wasn't stupid. She would have to lull him into believing she'd not only accepted her lot, but had come to embrace it.

I will beat you at your own game, she silently promised as James pulled the car to a stop in front of a large log cabin flanked by a screened-in porch. *And this time, when I get the gun, I won't be afraid to use it. And that's a promise.*

Chapter 9

James parked the car beneath the shade of a large tree with low-hanging branches and cut the engine. He released his seatbelt and then Kelsey's as well. "Welcome to your new home," he said with a peculiar smile that sent shivers of trepidation along Kelsey's spine. He opened his door and climbed out, moving out of Kelsey's line of vision as his shoes crunched on the gravel. A moment later he pulled open Kelsey's door. He crouched beside her and reached behind the seat to release the bungee cords.

A thousand stabbing needles of pain pricked her arms and hands as she pulled them forward onto her lap. She flexed her fingers and curled her hands into fists, wanting nothing more than to smash one into James' face.

He pulled her from the car and she saw he was holding the gun. The gravel was rough and warm beneath her bare feet and the wound on her leg had resumed its throbbing. It was hot outside and she was thirsty. She turned toward the cabin, expecting James to help her inside. Instead, to her extreme dismay, he pushed on her shoulders, forcing her to her knees on the dusty gravel.

"I want you, Kelsey. I want you so fucking bad." His voice was hoarse with lust and she saw the huge bulge of his erection beneath his shorts. With one hand, he tugged at his fly and pulled it open, while gripping a handful of her hair with the other. He pushed his shorts down to his knees to expose his cock and balls.

James leaned against the hood of the car and dragged her closer, pulling her up by the hair. "Suck my cock, baby. Do it good. Make me come like I made you come. And make sure you swallow every drop."

The head of his large cock was pressing insistently against her lips, his fingers twisting her hair so it tugged painfully against her scalp. "Do it," he urged, an angry tone now edging his voice. Without choice, Kelsey let her lips part, and James' thick, heavy cock slid into her mouth. He groaned with pleasure, loosening his grip somewhat on her hair. She had a brief fantasy of biting down so hard she bit it off, but even if she'd dared, it was shoved so far down her throat she couldn't close her mouth.

She heard the clunk of metal on metal and then felt his second hand on her head, holding her still while he fucked her face. She struggled not to gag as he slid in and out of her mouth and it was hard to breathe with the constant onslaught. The small rocks beneath her knees were digging painfully into her skin.

The gun, she thought suddenly. *That was the sound I heard. He set it on the hood. Make him come and then make your move.* Infused with a sudden energy, Kelsey brought her hands to his crotch and forced herself to cup his balls. He groaned, his grip tightening in her hair. "Yeah, baby. That's it. Yeah."

He continued to rut into her mouth for another minute or so and then he stiffened and thrust hard, his bitter jism shooting down her throat. His grip eased in her hair and his hands fell away as he gave a deep, satisfied sigh.

A spurt of adrenaline propelled Kelsey to her feet. There it was, glinting darkly in the sun. Kelsey grabbed the gun before James even had a chance to open his eyes. Her heart was beating high in her throat. He opened his eyes slowly and stared at her. In another second he'd leap to life and try to grab the gun.

Not this time, motherfucker.

Her hands were shaking as she took a step back, but determination overrode fear. She clutched the gun and cocked the trigger. Aiming at his face, she imagined the bullet tearing through skin and bone and exiting the back of his head with a splatter of blood and brains.

She squeezed the trigger.

The gun clicked.

James smiled grimly.

Kelsey stared at him, baffled. Confusion, shock and dread collided in her head, short-circuiting her ability to process what was happening. Again she pulled the trigger, and still nothing happened. Acting off instinct, she threw the gun as hard as she could at James' head. He lifted an arm to deflect the weapon, which fell with a thud to the gravel.

"You stupid little bitch," he hissed as he lunged toward her, his shorts still down around his knees. In a moment he was on her, his hands closing hard over her wrists as he jerked her forward. "You are a very, very bad girl, Kelsey Anne." His tone was menacing, his eyes sparking with anger.

He kept one hand firmly on her wrist, using the other to reach into the car. He pulled out the bungee cords and grabbed her other wrist, jerking her arms roughly behind her back. He bound them tightly with the cords, while Kelsey struggled ineffectually against him.

"It wasn't loaded," she heard herself say in a faint voice.

"Of course it wasn't loaded, you nitwit. You've already made your murderous intent clear. Leaving the gun where you could reach it was a test—a test you failed. I guess you'll just have to pay the consequences."

He had something in his hand. As he held it before her, she saw it was a pocket knife. He flicked it open, revealing the sharp silver blade. Kelsey felt as if all the breath had been sucked from her body.

But instead of slitting her throat, James hoisted her face-down over the hood of the car. "When I was kid," he said, his voice breathless with exertion, "if we misbehaved, our dad would punish us the old-fashioned way, with a birch switch. He used to make us go out and pick our own switch before supper. You would sit through the meal trying to choke down your food, scared out of your skin about what was coming."

Kelsey's cheek rested on the hot metal of the hood. She was too paralyzed with fear to move as James reached up and cut a long, thin branch from the tree. She could hear him stripping off the leaves and twigs.

"You're lucky," he said from behind her. She felt him step back and wondered if she could manage to get away somehow. "You don't have to wait through a meal of overcooked chicken and boiled peas. I'm going to whip your behind right here and now, you bad, bad girl."

The switch whistled through the air and bit into the backs of her thighs, leaving a searing sting in its wake. Kelsey screamed. The next blow hit her squarely across both ass cheeks. She screamed again and tried to roll away, but James' firm hand on her back stopped her.

"Naughty girl. You just lie there and take what's coming to you. It's okay to scream, though. No one will hear you. It's only you and me, babe. Just you and me." He struck her again and again until she felt as if her skin were being flayed from her body. She struggled and cried out with each biting stroke but James just kept on, and on, and on, until all the fight went out of her.

She lay limp and sobbing as the whippy rod continued to slash over her ass and thighs. Finally, finally, the beating stopped. Her body was bathed in sweat, the salt stinging her abraded flesh. She felt something warm and wet rolling down her legs and realized with dizzying horror that it was blood.

~*~

James dropped the switch and crouched behind Kelsey, staring in fascination at the welts he'd raised, his eyes tracking the slow roll of bright red blood where the branch had cut her soft white skin. He hadn't meant to hit her quite so hard or for quite so long. Though it had been over a decade since he'd felt the cut of the switch, James still remembered its fiery sting. But his father had never made him bleed.

But then, he'd never tried to shoot his father in the face, either. Kelsey had tried to kill him! In cold blood, she'd pulled that trigger, fully prepared to murder him. The thought was too much to handle just then, so he pushed it away, focusing instead on the rivulets of blood that trailed along her welted thighs.

He had done that. He had chastised his naughty girl with a beating, and now he would find a way to forgive her.

He realized his cock had returned to a rock-hard state, despite his having just orgasmed. He leaned forward and parted his lips, licking her skin as his cock throbbed. He drew his tongue down her leg, tasting the warm copper of blood mingled with the salt of her sweat.

I write the rules, he told himself, refusing to allow himself to be shocked at his behavior. *We've left the world behind us now, well and truly. My word is law. Kelsey lives or dies by my hand.* The thought thrilled him, power surging through his blood like a drug.

Kelsey was crying quietly, the tumble of her hair hiding her face as she rested against the hood of the car, her feet barely touching the ground. She looked so fucking hot like that, naked, arms bound behind her back, her ass and thighs welted and bleeding. Though he'd planned to take her inside and make love to her in the master bedroom, he realized he couldn't even wait as long as it would take to get her there.

Standing, he unzipped his shorts and pushed them down his legs, kicking them away. He grabbed her hips, lifting her to the proper angle as he nudged his aching cock between her legs. He brought one hand to his mouth and spit on his fingers. He reached for his cock with that hand and guided it to her tight entrance.

She stiffened at his touch. "No!" she whimpered through her snuffling tears.

"Yes," he replied. She squealed as he pushed his way inside her velvet heat. He felt like a god, powerful and dominant, completely in control. How dare she resist him? That would have to change. He would beat it out of her. He could see now that was the only way.

He pulled her fully onto his shaft, groaning with pleasure as her vaginal muscles massaged him. Her skin was hot to the touch. He looked down, watching his cock slide in and out of her. The sight filled him with fiery lust and he began to pummel her savagely.

"Bad girl," he grunted breathlessly as he rode her. "Bad, bad girl." His balls tightened and he knew he was seconds away from exploding. He looked down again at their conjoined bodies. He pulled out just as the spurting began, adding the cream of his ejaculate to the blood and sweat glistening on her welted ass and thighs.

When his heart had slowed and his head had cleared, he let go of the bound girl and took a step back. As he pulled his shorts back on and zipped them, he saw that fresh blood had seeped through the bandage on her calf. She lay limply over the hood of the car and, now that the bloodlust of his desire had eased away, James felt a rush of remorse.

Quickly he leaned over her and released the cords that bound her arms, which fell lifelessly against the hood. She didn't move. She didn't even appear to be breathing, and for a heart-stopping moment he thought she was dead.

He leaned over her again and put his face close to hers. Relief flooded him when he felt the soft rise and fall of her breathing. Gently, he reached beneath her and lifted her as he stood upright. Her eyes were closed, but they opened as he maneuvered her into his arms.

He carried her along the path and up the porch stairs to the front door. He had to set her down as he reached for his keys and unlocked the door, though he kept one arm securely around her shoulders so she wouldn't fall as she leaned heavily against him. He pushed open the door and deactivated the alarm.

The air was close and musty, but once he got the air conditioner going, it would be fine. Again he lifted his darling into his arms and carried her through the living room into the master bedroom.

In the few times he'd visited the cabin since his mother had died, he'd always stayed in the room he and his sister had shared when they were kids on their summer vacations, but that wouldn't do, not now that he had Kelsey with him. He was master of the house. Kelsey might be his unwilling captive for now. In time, though, he'd teach her to be his lover, his soulmate, his wife.

Once they might have been equals, back in that other life, under others' rules, but all that had changed now. Kelsey had left him no choice. Now it was up to him to help her understand that a man needed to exert a firm hand to teach his woman her place in his world. Once she understood that, they would explore the new frontier of their love together, far from the prying eyes of others.

He laid her gently on her stomach on the bare mattress, not even minding if she stained it. Soon he would cover it with fresh sheets. "You rest while the tub fills," he said to her back. She didn't respond. He sat next to her and stroked the hair from her face. "Kelsey. Look at me." She turned her head and fixed her large green eyes on his face. Her cheeks were flushed and damp with tears. Christ, she was beautiful.

"Kelsey, listen to me. I want you to understand something. You did a very bad thing, and you were punished, and now it's over. You are forgiven. I still love you. There's nothing you can do that would make me stop loving you." He waited a beat, half hoping she would respond in kind. She didn't.

She didn't love him.

Not yet.

That would come, in time. He understood now that his love alone was not enough to penetrate her sweet but thick head. She needed concrete lessons, and the switching he'd given her was only the beginning. He would break her down, wiping away her ego and her resistance. Only then could he build her up into the woman of his dreams. Only then could he claim her as the love of his life, and he of hers. They had time. All the time in the world.

"You're going to stay put while I run the bath, right? You're not going to try anything stupid again, are you?"

Slowly she shook her head.

James nodded. She looked too spent to try another escape, and anyway, he was bigger, stronger and faster. Still, why take chances? "I'm going to set the alarm. If you try to open a window or an outer door, it will trigger the alarm. You don't want to do that, Kelsey," he informed her. She didn't react. She was exhausted, poor thing.

He stood and stared down at her a moment, examining her ass and thighs. Yes, it had been a thorough whipping, but she'd be fine. The cuts were superficial, though there would probably be some bruising. He shrugged philosophically. Now she would think twice before she tried anything stupid again.

He set the alarm and then went into the bathroom to fill the tub. He added some bath oil he found in the cabinets and pulled out some towels. When he came back into the bedroom, Kelsey hadn't appeared to have moved at all.

He went to the kitchen to check out the provisions. The refrigerator was empty, but in the pantry he found cans of soup, a package of pasta and some spaghetti sauce, along with an unopened package of saltine crackers and a can of Cheez Whiz. He reached for the crackers and cheese. He put these on a serving tray, along with a glass of water, and returned to the bedroom.

Kelsey had shifted to her side, he was pleased to note. She watched him silently as he entered the room. He set the tray down and approached her. "Can you stand?" he asked solicitously. "I'll help you to the bathroom."

She didn't answer.

"Kelsey," he said sharply. "You will speak when spoken to. I know you don't want another switching…" He let the sentence hang as he glared at her.

That got her attention. She struggled into an upright position, wincing as her bottom touched the mattress. "Yes," she said, so quietly he had to strain to hear her. "I can stand."

"Good." He helped her upright and put an arm around her back for support. "Come into the bathroom and I'll feed you while you soak in the tub." He led her to the bathroom and let her pee. When she was done, he pulled the T-shirt over her head and crouched in front of her to remove the soiled bandage. "The wound is healing nicely, in spite of everything," he informed her with a smile.

Again she said nothing. Annoyed, James pressed the issue. "That's good, right?"

"Yes," she said in a flat tone.

James decided that would do for now. He stood and helped her into the tub. She stepped gingerly into the hot water, biting her lip as she lowered herself into it. While she settled in, James opened the saltines and pulled out a handful, setting them in a neat formation on the plate. He shook the Cheez Whiz can and squirted a circle of orange goo onto each cracker. He popped one into his mouth and chewed. It wasn't half bad.

He saw that Kelsey was watching him from the tub. "Hungry?" he said, aware she had to be.

She nodded. He lifted his eyebrows warningly and was pleased when she added, "Yes. And thirsty."

James held the glass of cold water to her lips and let her drink. When she'd finished nearly half the glass, he offered her a cracker. "It's up to you now, Kelsey," he informed her. "Good girls get to eat and drink. Bad girls go without their supper. Really bad girls get a whipping."

Her eyes widened, but she said nothing.

"Good girls respond when spoken to, as a sign of respect. In fact," James said, a sudden idea taking hold, "from this minute going forward, every time you address me, *every* time, Kelsey, you will call me sir, or you'll be punished. Are we clear on this, young lady?"

Kelsey pressed her lips together. He watched the cloud of fury pass over her features. She was a feisty one, make no mistake, but he loved that about her. He didn't want to destroy that spirit, but only to bend it to his will. He waited. He would count to three in his mind. If she didn't answer by then, and answer properly—

"Yes, sir," she said. It sounded as if the words had been forced past clenched teeth, but he liked the sound of them nonetheless.

"Say it again, Kelsey," he ordered. "Say it like you mean it."

Her green eyes flashed. James tilted his head at his naked captive, waiting.

"Yes, sir," she finally repeated.

James smiled.

Chapter 10

Kelsey turned onto her side on the bed, the cold chain clinking as she tucked her hands between her knees. Her wrists were wrapped in leather cuffs that were clipped to long, sturdy lengths of chain, which James had wound around the post of the four-poster bed.

Her ass and thighs still stung from the beating, and the wound on her calf was itching like crazy, but at least there was some give in the chains. When he'd gone out earlier that morning, he'd cuffed her wrist directly to one of the posts and left her that way, with her arms uncomfortably over her head.

She could hear him moving about in the kitchen of the small cabin, whistling while he clanked pots and slammed cabinet doors. The smell of fresh brewing coffee and sizzling bacon reached her nostrils, and she realized she was starving, the handful of crackers and cheese he'd given her the day before only a distant memory.

They'd gone to bed soon after her bath. James had insisted on drying her, and then re-bandaging her leg. He'd even insisted on brushing her teeth, forcing her to place her hands behind her head while he did so. She'd wanted to scream. She'd wanted to hit him. Instead she'd stood there, passive and unresisting, too afraid of him to protest.

Once in bed, James had wrapped her in a bear hug and pulled her close against his bare chest. Though he had fallen quickly asleep, Kelsey lay awake a long time in his tight embrace, plotting how she might escape. She needed to pretend to play along. She had to stop balking as she had been doing, as hard as that would be. She had to lull him into a false sense of security, enough so he would let his guard down, at least a little. Then she would find something she could use as a weapon. He'd brought the gun with him, after all. Maybe he'd brought the bullets too. There was that pocket knife he'd produced to cut the switch, or she could get hold of a kitchen knife.

If you'd asked her a week before if she could cut someone with a knife, she would have insisted she could not. Now, however, she knew she could—and would. She would slit the bastard's throat while he slept, grab his car keys and hightail it the hell out of there.

She didn't think she would sleep at all that night, but somehow she had, because she woke to find James standing over her, his hair wet from a shower, a small towel wrapped around his waist. She could see by the pale pink color of the sky outside the window that it was barely dawn.

He'd let her pee, though he stood there watching like the creep he was, and refused even to let her wipe herself, instead reaching his hand between her legs with a wad of toilet paper. "Though I have forgiven you for trying to kill me," he informed her as he pulled her to her feet, "you are still in disgrace. It's up to you how fast you win back basic privileges. You're going to need to show me that you are repentant and ready to obey me. Is that understood, Kelsey?"

She'd made the mistake of staring at him, open-mouthed with dismay and disbelief. That had earned her a slap across the face and a stern reminder. "How do you address me? Let's try again." James had glared at her and then repeated, speaking slowly as if to a stupid child, "Is that understood, Kelsey?"

"Yes, sir," she'd managed through gritted teeth.

Now James came into the bedroom carrying an old-fashioned TV tray with its own metal stand. Kelsey had to swallow the saliva pooling in her mouth at the sight of the plate heaped with food, and her empty stomach roiled with anticipation. He sat the tray on its stand beside the bed. There was a mug of steaming coffee, a plate of scrambled eggs and bacon and a bowl of something gray and gloppy.

"Ready for breakfast?" James asked with a smile.

I'm ready to fucking kill you. "Yes, please, sir," Kelsey managed, her taste buds already anticipating the salty crunch of the bacon and the soft, buttery-looking eggs.

"I'll remove the chains if you promise to behave. Do you promise?"

"Yes, sir."

Using a small key, he unlocked the cuffs and pulled them from her wrists. He put his arms supportively around her as she sat up, and she had to resist the strong urge to elbow him away. Let him think she was weaker than she was.

He sat beside her and reached for the mug of coffee, which she now saw was black. There was no second mug. He took a sip and set it back down. He picked up a piece of bacon and bit off half of it. He scooped up a forkful of eggs and shoveled it into his mouth. He continued to eat without looking at her. Kelsey's mouth continued to water as she waited impatiently for him to give her some.

Finally he looked at her, but instead of offering her bacon and eggs, he picked up the spoon and dipped it into the bowl. He brought a spoonful of thick oatmeal to Kelsey's lips. Kelsey felt her gorge rise and she pressed her lips together, angling her head away. The spoon followed her, a blob of the warm cereal falling onto her thigh.

"Open up, Kelsey. I know you're hungry."

She looked back at James, trying to keep the anger she felt from showing on her face as she flicked the offending goo from her leg. He had obviously done this on purpose, the prick. "I don't like oatmeal."

James's lips lifted in a cruel smile and he shrugged. "Good girls get eggs and bacon. Are you a good girl, Kelsey?"

She sensed a trap, but her empty stomach propelled her to say, "Yes, sir."

James lifted his eyebrows, a skeptical expression on his face. "Good girls do what they're told, when they're told. Good girls don't struggle and resist. Good girls don't aim guns at people's heads and pull the trigger."

Good boys don't tie women down and beat them till they bleed. Kelsey pressed her lips together and swallowed hard to keep from screaming.

"Are you ready to try and be a good girl, Kelsey?"

She dug her nails into her palms to keep from smashing her fists into his smug face. "Yes, sir."

James put down the spoon and reached for the fork. He scooped a mound of scrambled eggs onto it and brought the fork to her lips. But when Kelsey opened her mouth, he pulled the fork away, putting the food into his own mouth instead.

"Hey," she blurted, outraged and confused.

"Is for horses," James quipped. "Is there a problem, Kelsey?"

"Yes!" she cried, as he stuffed another piece of bacon into his mouth. "You said I could have some of that if I said I was a good girl. I really hate oatmeal. I want some eggs and bacon. And some coffee. Please? Please, sir?"

James shook his head. "You didn't listen. I didn't say you could have this food just for *saying* you're a good girl. You're going to have to prove you're a good girl before you earn the right to eat what you like. I'll give you ample opportunity to redeem yourself, I promise you." He lifted the spoon again, heaped with a gelatinous blob of gray mush. "Meanwhile, it's oatmeal or nothing."

Tears of fury and frustration burned behind Kelsey's eyes, but she blinked them away, refusing to give him the satisfaction. The congealed mess on the spoon turned her stomach, but Kelsey knew she had to eat. Closing her eyes, she opened her mouth.

James tipped the contents of the spoon into her mouth. He hadn't even bothered to add sugar or cream, and the oatmeal had the consistency of wet cement, but Kelsey forced herself to swallow it. She managed to get down three more spoonfuls before turning her head away.

"You had enough?" James asked.

"Yes, sir," Kelsey said, though she was still starving. If anything, the bit of food made her feel hungrier than before, and her head ached, probably from lack of caffeine. "May I have some coffee, sir?" she said, trying to keep her tone meek and sweet.

James lifted his mug to his lips and took a long swallow. "No. Only good girls get coffee." He set the mug on the tray and stood. "Now." He put his hands on his hips as he stared down at her. "Here's your first chance to show me what a good girl you're going to be from now on. It's time to shave that sweet little cunt of yours. I expect you to cooperate fully during the process. If you please me, you might have something other than oatmeal at lunch time. If not..." he didn't finish the sentence, but the threat was clear.

Instinctively Kelsey put her hand protectively over her pubic mound. Adam had wanted her to shave, and she had said she would if he would, which had ended that particular conversation. Obviously James wasn't asking her opinion on the matter.

The idea of another person drawing a razor over her private parts, especially a man who had already demonstrated he didn't mind spilling her blood, made Kelsey shudder with trepidation. On the other hand, if she submitted to this demand she could begin the process of fooling James into thinking she was going along with his insanity. And it wasn't as if she really had a choice anyway. He would do what he wanted, and she could come along quietly, or kicking and screaming. That was really all the choice left to her.

When he held out his hand, Kelsey took it, allowing him to pull her upright. She was pleased to see she could put a little more weight on her wounded leg than before, but distressed at how weak she felt overall. Was that part of his devious master plan—to keep her weak and hungry, and thus easier to control?

The man was a monster, but that monster held her life in his hands.

For now.

~*~

Sitting at the small desk in the corner of the room, James stroked his cock, silently congratulating himself on keeping the satellite internet service going for the cabin, even though he hadn't come here all that often. Laptop open, he scrolled through the websites on his chosen topic, astonished to find out just how many there were. "This is a whole lifestyle," he called out to Kelsey, who lay so prettily across the room on the bed in chains, her bare, naked cunt elevated by the pillows he'd placed beneath her ass, her legs spread wide so he could gaze at the sweet pink labia now so visible between her thighs.

After he'd shaved her cunt, being oh-so-careful with the razor on her tender nether lips, he'd squirted plenty of baby oil over her sex until it glistened, having seen someone do that on a porn site. He liked the way it looked, all pink and shiny with oil, and so he'd left it that way when he helped her back onto the bed and chained her down.

His research was going well. He was looking for guidance in this new lifestyle he'd chosen for them, but hadn't expected to find such a wealth of information. There were literally dozens of websites devoted to offering guidance and support to men and women interested in developing a relationship where the man is fully in charge and the woman knows her place. There were lots of useful, practical tips to create the correct environment, like making sure there was a specific punishment spot where a disobedient wife could contemplate the errors of her ways. James had decided on the bedroom closet. He'd added a sliding bolt to the outside of the door so he could lock Kelsey inside when she misbehaved.

"Listen to this from this blog." He read aloud, "*I am usually a good wife. I get my share of beatings, but they are always deserved, and I learn from them and try harder. Obedience is something my husband insists on and I am mostly good at it. Then came the day I decided to blow off the housework and grocery shopping to spend the day at the movies with a girlfriend.*

"*When I got home, my husband was waiting with his belt in his hands, a frown on his handsome face. 'Why are there dishes in the sink?' he asked in that deep, quiet voice of his.*

"*I began to tremble. 'I — I went to the movies with Susan. I didn't realize I'd be so late.'*

"*'And where is dinner?' My husband glared at the greasy bag of takeout food I held in my hand. 'Don't tell me* that's dinner, after I worked hard all day to make money to take care of you.'

"I swallowed hard and nodded, a tear rolling down my cheek. My husband pointed to the floor at his feet and I knew what to do. I quickly pulled off my blouse and skirt, glad at least I had on my sexy underwear and matching bra underneath. Since we've adopted this lifestyle, I threw out all my cotton undies and only wear silk and lace for my Sir.

"'All of it,' he said sternly, waiting while I peeled off my underwear and removed my bra. 'Punishment position, ass up,' he ordered.

"I knelt hurriedly at his feet, my hands stretched out on the cold marble floor of our foyer, ass offered for his belt. He hit me hard, each stroke stinging like crazy as the slapping sound echoed off the walls. I was crying by the time he was done. He let me turn around and kiss his shoes and then he pulled me up into his arms and kissed away the tears.

"I begged him to let me worship his cock before I went to cook him a proper dinner. He pulled open his pants, pushed me to my knees, and let me suck his beautiful cock and balls. He didn't allow me to swallow, though, because only good girls get to swallow their Sir's cum. Instead he spurted on my face and breasts. I had to leave it there to dry while I cooked dinner, and while we ate, as a reminder of my sins."

As he read the woman's testimonial to Kelsey, James' cock got so hard it started leaking fluid from the tip. He'd had no idea there were so many people actually living this kind of lifestyle. And yes, this was what he wanted—not some Master/slave kink fest with black leather and red walls, but a husband/wife relationship based on man's natural dominance and woman's natural submission. A lifetime of behaving politically correctly and mouthing all the right words about women's rights and liberation had fallen by the wayside the night he'd thrown Kelsey into his car. The real James Bennett had emerged, strong and powerful and ready to take his due.

He bookmarked the page and stood, closing the lid of the laptop. He turned to the lovely, naked girl chained on his bed. He wanted to fuck her, but first he wanted to play with her naked little cunt.

He had laid their small collection of sex toys on the shelf built into the wall on the side of the bed. He sat beside Kelsey and reached across her for her vibrator. Her cunt was still glistening with baby oil, so he decided to dispense with additional lubricant. "Spread your legs wider," he ordered, smacking lightly at her thigh. He eased the phallus into her tight cunt, excited by her little cries and gasps.

When it was fully inside her, he turned it on high. He stroked his cock as he watched, until he realized the thing was vibrating itself out of her. That wouldn't do, and he pushed it back in with the hand not holding his shaft.

Then he had a better idea.

"You ever been fucked up the ass, Kelsey?"

She didn't answer right away, and he tore away his gaze from her sex to look at her face. "I asked a question," he said warningly.

"Yes, sir," she answered.

This annoyed him. He'd wanted to be her first. Who had taken her anal virginity? That Adam guy she was with in college? That dick Steve Hardin? Never mind. It didn't matter. He would forgive her for every guy she'd ever been with. She belonged to him now, and him alone.

He pulled the vibrator out of her and set it carefully upright on the shelf. He reached for the lanyard he now wore around his neck, on which he'd placed the padlock keys to her cuffs. Leaning forward, he released her wrists cuffs, leaving them dangling from the chains so he could lock her up again when he was done with her.

"Turn over," he said brusquely. "On your hands and knees. I'm going to fuck your ass." He didn't admit he himself was in fact the virgin in this particular equation. He'd wanted to have anal sex with Emily, but the bitch had refused him. Kelsey wouldn't refuse him, though. She wouldn't dare.

He watched with satisfaction as she rolled over and pulled herself up on her hands and knees. He crouched behind her, his cock bobbing at full erection.

"While I fuck your ass, your job is to make sure that vibrator stays inside your cunt. You hold it in place. If it falls out, I'll have to punish you."

She twisted her head back to face him, the fear ripe in her clear green eyes. "Please, James, I don't want—"

"I didn't tell you to speak, Kelsey!" James shouted over her. He would have to write up a list of rules for her like he saw on so many of those training sites. Number one would be: no talking unless asked a direct question.

She turned her head forward again and hunched her shoulders. She made a snuffling sound. He realized she might be crying, and his heart seized suddenly with pity. What was he doing?

Then he remembered the hatred that had twisted her features into something ugly as she'd pointed the gun at him, ready to shoot him at point blank range, and his heart hardened. He grabbed the vibrator from the shelf and pushed it back inside the girl. "Hold on to it," he commanded as he flicked it to high. He smacked one welted ass cheek for emphasis. "Go on, do it. Now."

He was pleased when she obeyed, reaching back and covering the base of the vibrator with her fingers. How many lonely nights had she fucked herself with that thing, while dreaming of her one true love?

"He's here now," James wanted to say, but of course he did not. She wouldn't believe it. Not yet.

He reached for the tube of lubricant from the shelf and rubbed it on the head of his cock, smearing the excess left on his fingers over the tight bud of her asshole. She pulled away from his touch. "Don't move," he ordered tersely.

He touched her asshole with the tip of his finger and then pushed it in to the first knuckle. "Relax," he soothed. "It'll be a lot easier if you can relax." He pushed his finger in to the second knuckle. Kelsey yelped and jerked again. James ignored this as he moved his finger, working to relax her sphincter muscles. He would hold her still while he fucked her.

He withdrew his finger and positioned himself between her legs. When he nudged the head of his lubricated cock between her cheeks, Kelsey's hand fell away from the vibrator as she jerked forward.

"Damn it, Kelsey. I'm warning you. Get back in position. Hold that thing in place." He waited, silently counting until she reached again for the dildo. "Good girl," he said encouragingly, pleased he'd only had to count to two. "Now, just relax."

He nudged again against her sphincter with his cock, and pushed past the ring of muscle. Kelsey grunted, but stayed in position. As James eased himself into her ass, he could feel the vibrator's girth pressing against the thin membrane that separated her rectum from her cunt.

Fucking her ass was different from fucking her cunt, which hugged his shaft like a warm velvet glove. This felt more like a tight band that stroked his cock as he moved in and out, and the vibrations from the dildo made the experience all the more intense.

Kelsey cried out as he pushed himself deeper inside her ass. He gripped her hips and began to thrust in and out of the tight, hot hole. She was being a good girl, her fingers still curled around the base of the vibrator in spite the awkwardness of her position.

James felt alive, his whole being thrumming in time with the vibrations radiating from her cunt and swirling over his sheathed cock. His heart was hammering, his breath ragged in his throat as he fucked his girl, slamming in and out of her. He wanted to hold on longer to savor the intensity of the experience, but knew it was hopeless.

Within minutes he felt the tightening in his balls that signaled an orgasm and he let it go, exploding inside the tight heat of Kelsey's ass. He fell forward against her and she collapsed beneath him, the vibrator continuing to hum. Still inside her, James rolled to his side, pulling her with him. He reached between her legs and pulled out the vibrator, which he turned off and dropped over the side of the bed.

He pulled Kelsey against him, finding and cupping her small, firm breasts. He could feel her heart thumping and the rise and fall of her chest. Had she climaxed? His cock twitched at the notion. She was so fucking hot!

"Kelsey," he murmured, nuzzling his face into her thick, soft hair. "I love you."

She didn't answer.

Chapter 11

A cool breeze wafted through the porch screen. The lake water looked especially blue in the distance, a sailboat drifting lazily on its surface. Would James ever let her go down to the water? Would she ever be allowed beyond the confines of the cabin?

Since he'd brought her to the cabin, she'd earned privileges, bit by bit. At first it had been hard—so hard—to force herself to call him sir, and to submit to his demands and punishments without wanting to scratch his eyes out.

It wasn't as hard now. Sometimes she was startled to realize she hadn't even thought about escape for hours on end. Her focus was more on staying out of the punishment closet, avoiding pain and earning privileges.

She still had plans of escape, make no mistake, but for now it was better to adapt. As twisted as he was, James really did love her, in his way. It was easier to focus on the love, rather than the torturous path he drew her along to receive that love.

Kelsey cradled the warm coffee mug in her hands and sipped the strong, delicious brew. As always, James had added just the right amount of cream and sugar. She loved being allowed to hold the mug herself—a recent privilege, though he still insisted on feeding her.

She'd been so grateful when, after two solid days of disgusting oatmeal, he'd permitted her to share his meal—a perfectly cooked steak and a fresh spinach salad. Each bite had been like heaven in her mouth, and he'd let her eat until she was full.

There had only been one day where she'd been denied food and water. That had been tough. She'd spent most of that day locked inside the punishment closet, sweating in the close confines of the small, hot space, and trying not to freak out. She had learned it was better not to beg to be let out—that only made the punishment last longer. Since then, she'd only spent a few minutes in the closet from time to time, and she'd never missed a meal, though he never let her eat as much as she wanted.

She would have loved at least a few more bites of the French toast he'd prepared for their breakfast that morning, but half a piece had been all he'd allowed her. He'd eaten three pieces himself, along with three slices of bacon. There was still a piece of bacon and the other half of her French toast on the plate, but Kelsey knew better than to ask for it.

"I wouldn't want you to get fat," he'd explained. "It's important that you maintain your appearance for me, but it goes deeper than that. I read on the *Her Husband's Hard Hand* that a wife should never be permitted to overeat. A wife needs to understand that she is subservient to her husband, and staying hungry is a keen reminder that she serves at her husband's pleasure."

James loved all those websites about training and discipline, and read to her daily from the blogs. At first she'd been horrified to think there were so many deluded women out there, perfectly ready, even eager, to bend their will to a man. Now, though, she was getting more used to the idea. After all, what choice did she have?

She wasn't his wife, but he called her that all the time anyway. "We're married in spirit," he'd claimed. "One day, when you prove yourself worthy, we'll marry in the eyes of the law as well. I hope you can earn that honor someday, Kelsey. Until then, I'll continue to train and guide you on your journey along the path of a properly submissive woman."

Kelsey glanced in James' direction as she stroked her leather wrist cuffs. He was watching her, she realized suddenly, his gray eyes moving from her face to her bare breasts as the tip of his tongue appeared between his lips. She knew that sign. Soon she would be on her knees, his cock down her throat. Then would come her morning chores. Her leg had healed so well, she barely limped now as she moved through the cabin dusting the furniture and shelves, sweeping and cleaning the floors. She enjoyed doing her chores, if for no other reason than he left her alone while she was working, though he was always nearby. Each day she set herself a personal challenge to do every chore just right so he wouldn't have to punish her. So far, though, she had failed every time. No matter how well she thought she had done, he always found fault with something.

Aware of his gaze on her, Kelsey set down her mug and lowered her eyes submissively, as she knew he liked, waiting for the command to kneel at his feet.

Instead, to her surprise, he said, "I was thinking maybe it's time we started our own blog. *James' Obedient Wife.* That has a nice ring to it. I'm thinking we would post a photograph of you, too, to draw interest. Not your face of course," he said quickly. "I'm thinking maybe one of that delectable ass of yours, whipped to a nice cherry red. That would please me. What do you think?"

Kelsey swallowed, searching in her mind for the trick in the question. She didn't want to have a picture of her naked body posted on the internet, but she also understood he wasn't asking if she agreed or not to his plans, but rather, how she felt about what was going to happen, with or without her consent. She didn't want a spanking either, or a whipping.

Answer truthfully. Always answer truthfully, as a good wife should. I'll know when you're lying, Kelsey. A husband always knows.

The scary thing was, he usually did know.

But not always.

She'd been getting better at keeping her feelings more tightly coiled deep inside her, hidden behind a mask of serene obedience. When she succeeded, he rewarded her with hot coffee, food, warm baths and orgasms. Lots of orgasms.

When she failed, however, the punishments were swift and severe.

"I—I don't want a whipping, sir. I've been a good girl. Haven't I?"

"Up until this moment, yes," he agreed pleasantly, though she didn't like the sudden cruel curve of his smile, or the glint in his eye. "But good girls don't state their opinions about whether they want whippings or not. Surely you know that by now, wife?"

Kelsey's gut clenched and she bit her lower lip. Fuck. When he started calling her wife, she was usually in trouble. "Yes, sir. I'm sorry, sir," she said quickly.

James stood, and she saw the erection tenting his shorts. He shook his head, making a "tsking" sound. "You had been doing so well, but you forgot one of the prime rules of wifely submission. A wife doesn't voice what she does or does not want. She asks what would please her husband, and no more." He frowned, though his cock continued to strain at his shorts.

"Go on," he insisted, "tell me. What would the proper response have been to my question?"

Kelsey felt tears pricking her eyelids. Damn it, she should have known the answer—why had she fucked it up? "If—if it pleases you, sir, then it pleases me."

James reached for her arm and jerked her up from the chair. "That's better. You're mouthing the words at least, though it's clear it's not yet a part of your psyche. I'll just have to work harder." He walked toward the door, pulling her along with him. "Come on. Punishment time."

He led her to the center of the living room and stopped, still gripping her arm. "I guess that's what comes of sparing the rod," he said with an exaggerated sigh. "An article I read recently said a husband should discipline his wife daily, as a constant reminder that she is cherished. It shows he cares enough to take her in hand. It said men often make the mistake of being too soft on their wives, and then the woman doesn't trust or understand the true extent of her husband's natural authority, or his duty to exert total control. I've been remiss. I think we'll rectify that today, Kelsey. Stand under the beam and raise your arms over your head."

The large, open living room that comprised most of the cabin's space had thick exposed wooden support beams suspended below the cathedral ceiling. Early in their stay James had thrown sturdy ropes over the center beam, where they had remained, a constant warning.

Something about being bound by the wrists by that rough, scratchy rope, arms spread wide and pulled taut so she was forced on tiptoe, made Kelsey feel more vulnerable and frightened than any other kind of punishment. There was no way to hide, no way to shield any part of her body from his switch, his whip or his hand.

Kelsey shivered with fear as James removed her cuffs so he could tie the rope directly around her wrists. She knew from experience the ropes would burn and chafe her skin if she wriggled too much. He adjusted the ropes, pulling at them until she was forced onto her toes. He left the room a moment. When he returned, he was naked, his cock jutting hard and thick from his body, the whip in his hand.

He'd only used the whip twice before, and she been marked afterwards each time, though no more so than from a hard spanking. But something about the whip itself frightened her in a way she couldn't quite articulate. Maybe it was because the person wielding it had no direct contact of skin on skin, as with a spanking, and so it became a less personal, more removed kind of interaction. How could James insist he cherished her while wielding a whip? It didn't make sense to her, not even within the framework of the obedient wife.

"Please," she blurted. "Not the whip. I've been a good girl." The words tumbled out before she could stop them. She bit her lip to keep from saying anymore, quailing as James' face darkened.

He reached for her throat, his strong, large hand closing over it. He squeezed as he said, "Did I ask you a question, wife?" Mutely, Kelsey shook her head, trying to keep her panic at bay as he squeezed harder. "Then keep that pretty mouth closed and take what's coming to you."

He let her go, and she swayed on her toes, the rough rope tight around her wrists. He stepped to the side. She could see him in her peripheral vision as he pulled back his whip arm. The first snap of the leather against her ass stung, but not as much as she'd feared.

I can do this, she told herself. *I can take the whip for James, and then he'll be pleased with me.*

The second stroke was harder than the first. It was followed by a series of short, sharp flicks, the tips of the leather tresses stinging like little bees over her ass. Kelsey began to dance on her toes as she struggled not to make a sound. James had taught her that the obedient wife does not cry and plea for mercy, but takes what is given in stoic silence.

He struck her again and again, until her ass and the backs of her thighs were on fire. In spite of herself, she began to whimper. She bit her lip and squeezed her eyes shut in her effort to stay silent.

Then he struck her back—hard.

As much from surprise as pain, Kelsey emitted a yelp as she tried to twist away from the stinging lash. Another blow landed squarely across her shoulders. He had never hit her before anywhere but her ass and thighs. The sting along her back was sharper and much harder to take.

"Silence, wife!" James shouted. He struck her back again and again until it stung as much as her ass ever had, and more. Somehow she managed to stay reasonably quiet after the first cry, though tears were coursing down her cheeks. All thoughts of pleasing James had fled. She just wanted to get through this.

Just when she thought she couldn't take another stroke, James appeared in front of her, his cock still rigid, a drop of pre-come wobbling at the tip. He pulled back his arm and let the lash snap over her bare breasts. Kelsey gasped in pain. He struck her again and one of the lash tips caught her directly on the right nipple. The pain was blinding and she screamed.

James slapped her across the face. "Silence!" he roared. He struck her breasts again and again until the tender skin felt flayed and torn. Though Kelsey bit her lip as hard as she could, she couldn't stop the whimpering cries that escaped. He had never whipped her for so long, or so brutally.

It wasn't fair! She was a good girl!

Finally, finally, he dropped the whip. "What do you say?" he demanded.

Tears were streaming down Kelsey's face and it was hard to catch her breath, but she knew what was expected, and that it would go worse for her if she didn't answer. "Thank you," she managed.

"What's that?" he snapped, frowning. "Aren't you forgetting something?"

"Sir!" she cried, panic making her squeak. "Thank you, *sir*."

He nodded and reached for her wrists. Kelsey hadn't realized how hard she'd been tugging on the rope, but she realized it now as James unknotted the restraints, and she both saw and felt the rope burns caused by her struggles.

It's over, it's over. Now he'll comfort me. He'll hold me and tell me he loves me. He'll run a hot bath for me and let me soak in water made fragrant with lavender bath oil.

But he didn't do that.

Instead he pushed her to the ground, forcing her onto her stomach against the wide-planked pinewood floor. Her skin was stinging from shoulder to thigh, her tender breasts mashed against the ground, her wrists throbbing. James crouched behind her, pulling her to her hands and knees while thrusting his cock into her. She felt the skin tearing at her entrance as he rammed himself inside her. He was grunting like a feral animal, his fingers digging hard into her hips.

"Kelsey, Kelsey, Kelsey," he chanted as he rutted inside her. At least the hard cock pummeling her offered some distraction from her torn, flayed skin. It was only a minute or so before he stiffened and then jerked, climaxing inside her with a cry.

Once he pulled out of her, Kelsey's instinct was to curl into a tight ball on the floor, but she felt James' strong arms go around her, and then she was lifted into the air and pulled close against his chest.

"I'm sorry I was so rough, darling," he whispered gruffly as he carried her toward the bedroom, "but it's the only way to tame that wild spirit of yours. It's for your own good, believe me."

He laid her on her stomach on the bed. She closed her eyes, hoping he would go away, though she knew better. She felt him sit beside her, and then his fingers moving lightly over her ass.

"This beating will leave some marks. You should think of them as badges of courage. It takes courage and grace to be an obedient, submissive wife. I'm really proud of you, Kelsey."

Badges of courage? How about badges of brutality?

A sudden black tide of unwelcome rage lapped at the edges of Kelsey's consciousness, threatening to spill over. *Peaceful thoughts. Let it go. Flow with the pain, focus on the good things. Don't let him see the anger. Don't let him know.* It took all her will to push away the negative feelings before James sensed them. The last thing she needed right now was another punishment. She just wanted to be left alone.

Thankfully, her mutinous thoughts remained hidden. A moment later she felt the cool salve he used on her skin after especially brutal beatings. His touch was gentle, and the soothing balm felt good as it penetrated the still-stinging skin of her ass, back and thighs. After a while he turned her over and rubbed more of the salve onto her breasts.

When he was done, he wrapped her cuffs around her wrists, covering the rope burns with the black leather. He clipped the cuffs to the headboard chains, unspooling them to their full length so she had maximum movement, which Kelsey appreciated.

"You take a rest. I'll wake you in time for lunch." James stroked her hair from her face and leaned down to kiss her cheek.

Kelsey closed her eyes and imagined herself slipping out of her aching body and floating up into a cloudless blue sky. She focused on emptying her mind and letting all thoughts, fear, pain and anguish fall away. She opened her arms, which had become wide, white wings, and flew away.

~*~

James placed the slices of turkey on the bread and reached for the mayonnaise jar. The warm afternoon sun was shining through the window and bathing the kitchen in a golden glow. A beautiful, sexy, submissive woman lay asleep in his bed. She belonged to him, and him alone. Life was good.

Since he'd started reading the obedient wife sites, a whole new world had opened up, one in which his natural inclinations and secret desires had a place. For the first time in his life, he felt like he fit in. He had found a community of like-minded individuals. He wasn't suffering from perverted or twisted thinking, as he had sometimes feared. There was a rooted basis in many religions and cultures for a man taking full control of his woman.

If he happened to derive great sexual satisfaction from exercising that control, where was the harm?

The harm is that she's here against her will. The harm is that this is a non-consensual relationship, no matter how you try to couch it in obedient wife theory or the natural order of things. You took her by force, and you keep her by force. Where is the love in that?

Angered, James shook away that small but unwelcome voice that still occasionally plagued him. That voice had no place in their lives now. As he'd told himself a thousand times, what was done was done. There was no going back. The old rules no longer applied. He'd written new rules, and they were working.

Kelsey had blossomed in just the short time they'd been together. Already she had learned many of the basic tenants of the obedient wife philosophy, and seemed to embrace them. She never asked him to let her go anymore, and she seemed genuinely thrilled when he praised her, her face glowing with happiness when he told her she'd been a good girl.

She'd never looked like that back in that other life, when they'd both spent their days crunching numbers in the back room of a huge, impersonal banking conglomerate that didn't give a shit if either of them lived or died. Though she'd been good at her job, she'd never beamed under his praise. Theirs had been a casual flirtation, nothing more.

Not so now. Now he was the center of her universe. She literally lived or died at his hand, and there was no greater high in this world.

James was amazed at how easily he'd let the life he'd lived before slip away. Until he'd met Kelsey, he'd honestly believed his career was the most important thing in his life. Though his sizable inheritance would have let him retire and never work again, he'd never even considered leaving his job before he met her. Badly burned by Emily's betrayal, he hadn't even thought about looking for another partner. Work had been everything, until Kelsey Anne Rowan had appeared in his life like a golden angel, lighting his world.

His life had new meaning now. He was training Kelsey to be his obedient, dutiful wife. All the research he'd done assured him that her love would come in time as a natural byproduct of the obedience and duty.

Already Kelsey was completely dependent on him for everything she did — he'd seen to that. He was the only person she saw or talked to, ever. She didn't eat unless he fed her. She didn't sleep until he gave her permission. She didn't use the toilet, or bathe or read a book unless he said she could. When he decided she'd earned a punishment, she bent over his knee or assumed a punishment position without hesitation and without question. And she thanked him afterwards, even through her tears.

Maybe he'd been too hard on her this morning, but he couldn't deny the deep, wild thrill he had gotten from whipping her all over and holding nothing back. He'd loved the sudden howl of shocked pain when he'd brought the whip down on her back and shoulders. He'd loved the way her perfect breasts jiggled with each blow of the whip, her nipples hard and red by the time he'd finished stimulating them with the stinging leather.

If he were honest, the whipping hadn't been about teaching her, or punishing her, not by the time he was done. It had been a kind of lovemaking really, the whip an extension of his cock, her entire body just a quivering cunt, *his* cunt, there solely to satisfy his lusts.

James was distracted from his thoughts by a sound coming from outside. It took him a second to register that it was car tires crunching on gravel. He couldn't see the driveway from the kitchen window. Dropping the mayonnaise knife, he sprinted into the living room toward the front windows that looked out on the porch and beyond to the driveway.

A nondescript black sedan was pulling up in front of the house. There were two men inside. *Don't panic. It's probably just salesmen or preachers or something,* he tried to tell himself. He glanced back at the bedroom door, which was ajar. His heart slamming into high gear, he sprinted across the room and glanced inside the door.

Kelsey was sleeping like an angel. James pulled the door closed with a click. As he turned around, he saw the ropes dangling from the beam and raced toward them, yanking them down and kicking them under the couch. Trying to slow his breathing, he ran his hands through his hair as he watched the men climb out of their car and lumber up to the screen door.

Deciding to seize the bull by the horns, he went out onto the porch and pulled open the screen door, hoping the smile he was aiming for made it to his face.

Before him stood two uniformed policemen.

The air thickened somehow, and James found himself unable to draw a breath. Sweat sprouted under his arms and beaded along his upper lip as he stood staring at the men, his mind suddenly, utterly and completely blank.

"James Bennett?" one of them said, while the other held out his badge.

James opened his mouth and managed to croak, "Yes?"

"May we come in a moment, sir?"

They hadn't pulled out a warrant for his arrest, at least not yet.

Feeling as if he were a fly trapped in amber, James somehow made his limbs move. He stepped back and gestured the men onto the porch. "What's the trouble, officers?"

"We're making inquiries into a possible missing person. Bob Reynolds gave us your name and address information. We called your cell phone a couple of times but it went to voice mail."

"Oh," James had forgotten that Reynolds knew about his cabin. "We get sporadic cell service out here sometimes," he offered lamely.

"We?" one of the officers, a heavy man in his forties with a buzz cut cocked an eyebrow.

Oh god. I'm dead. I'm dead. "A figure of speech," James found himself saying. "I mean service is sporadic around here. I'm alone here in the cabin."

Don't make a sound, Kelsey. Not a sound.

Sweat was rolling from his forehead into his eyes and James wiped at it with his hands.

"You okay, Mr. Bennett?" asked the younger cop, a thin, wiry man in his twenties.

"I—I'm fine. I'm sorry. I'm—I'm not feeling so good."

"Mr. Reynolds mentioned your condition." The cop's tone was sympathetic.

James seized on the man's words like a lifeline. "Yes," he agreed, hoping the tremble in his voice would be attributed to his "condition". "They've been really great at the bank, letting me take all the time I need. I haven't told them yet, but there's no cure. I haven't got that long left..." He trailed off, lifting his chin and offering what he hoped was a brave countenance in the face of impending death.

The two cops were staring at him, and he wondered suddenly if he'd laid it on a bit too thick. "Uh, I'm sorry." Again James took the bull by its horns. He would get through this and send these men packing. "You said you were here about a missing person? Someone from work?"

"Yeah," the beefy cop said, looking down at the pad in his hand. "Kelsey Rowan."

James' heart was beating so hard he was afraid the cops could hear it. He ran a hand over his face as he struggled to compose his thoughts. He looked up. "She's missing? She quit the bank a while back. It was the same day I started my leave, I remember now. She didn't give any notice. She just left a voice message. It was pretty shocking, really." He shrugged, making eye contact with the older cop. "Young people today..."

"Did she say where she was going? Did she have another job she was taking?"

James stared at the ceiling, pretending to think back. He shook his head. "No, not that I recall. Her parents are in Florida, I think. Maybe she went back there?"

"Nope. Her parents are the ones who made the report. Apparently she hasn't been back to her apartment for quite some time, and her cell goes straight to voice mail. We haven't been able to trace the phone's location. There's been no credit card use. Her rent's past due. Do you still have the voice message she left, by chance? They accessed your voicemail at work, but it wasn't there. Did she call your cell?"

"No, I'm sorry. We were just colleagues, nothing more than that. The call was on my work phone, but I routinely delete my voicemail messages as a matter of course. It didn't occur to me to save it, frankly." He blew out a breath and brought his hands to his face, silently praying the cops were buying his story.

The fat cop consulted his pad again. "Some of the bank employees we interviewed indicated you two were the last ones left at the group's happy hour. Ms. Rowan was seen leaving Sal's Pub on Thursday, July eleventh around eight o'clock with a man matching your description."

James' blood froze in his veins and for one horrible second he thought he was going to burst out crying. *Stop it. Get a hold of yourself. They don't know a fucking thing. They're just fishing for information.* James lifted his head and forced himself to meet the man's eye. "I remember that night. Some of the folks in the department had gone out for pizza and a beer. I gave Kelsey a ride to her bus stop afterward."

"You had a car parked at Sal's?" The cop frowned.

Stick to as much of the truth as you can. "No. I have a parking space in the car garage next to the bank. We walked down together and then I gave her a ride. She didn't say anything about quitting either. I didn't get that message until the next morning when I went into the office."

"Where did you drop her? What stop?"

James told them, silently congratulating himself that he knew exactly where Kelsey got on and off the bus, along with where she shopped for groceries, where she lived, and a whole lot more, not that he'd ever let them know that. Instead, he said, "Man, this is really awful. I hope nothing's happened to her. Yeah, she was irresponsible, but she was a sweet kid. If there's any way I can help..." He held out his hands, palms up and looked at each cop in turn.

"Keep your eyes and ears open," said the older cop as he hoisted himself to his feet. The young cop handed James a card. "If you hear anything or think of anything that might be useful, give us a call."

James took the card and shoved it into his pocket "I will," he promised. "Gosh, I hope you find her. I hope she's okay."

"You too," the younger cop said. "Hang in there."

"Yeah, thanks."

James walked the cops to the screen door, and watched as they got into their unmarked vehicle. The young cop climbed behind the wheel, while the fat one scribbled something on his pad. Finally they drove away.

James went back into the house and collapsed onto the couch. He felt as if he'd just run a marathon. His muscles had turned to jelly, his hands were shaking, his heart beating so fast he thought he might pass out.

He lay back against the couch, taking deep, slow breaths until he could calm himself down. Everything was okay. Those cops were just doing their duty, going through the motions, checking all the leads.

They hadn't even asked to come inside the house. He wasn't a suspect.

He realized now what a horrible, stupid risk he'd taken in going back to her apartment, but apparently no one had noticed his coming or going in that big, impersonal complex in which she had lived. He would be even more careful going forward. Kelsey's cell phone was in the trunk of his car, along with her purse. Thank goodness he'd thought to remove the cell battery. He would dispose of her things as soon as possible. He would hide them in a bag of garbage and take the bag to the local dump. He would make sure Kelsey never left the cabin. She wouldn't even be allowed on the screened-in porch anymore. At least not until this whole missing person thing had well and truly blown over.

Maybe he would change her name and color her hair. They could drive down to Texas or Mexico or somewhere and start a whole new life, where no one knew them. But for now he would lie low. It might look suspicious if he suddenly took off. He would touch base with Reynolds, let him know he was leaving the bank for good, and then bide his time until it was safe to move his precious cargo out of the state.

He sat up, feeling much better. He held out his hands in front of him, pleased to see they were steady as rocks. His breathing had returned to normal and he was no longer sweating. He'd handled things brilliantly with the cops. They hadn't suspected a thing. And Kelsey, darling Kelsey, wonderful Kelsey, hadn't made a peep. He would let her eat a whole sandwich for lunch, and a peach too.

He stood and moved toward the bedroom. Opening the door slowly, he peered in. She was lying on her side, her back toward him. Her lovely ass was crisscrossed with welts and there were even a few marks on her slender back and pretty shoulders.

He'd done that. He'd marked his property, while teaching her to accept her place as his obedient wife. They would start the blog entry right after lunch, he decided. Despite her little slipup earlier, he deemed her ready.

As he approached her, his cock twitched in anticipation. Reaching into his shorts, he stroked it, pleased to see it was already erect, despite his having fucked her only an hour ago, and despite the cops sending him into a temporary tailspin.

Everything was fine now. Better than fine. His eyes on his prize, he quickly stripped off his shirt and shorts. He approached the bed and reached for Kelsey's shoulder, pulling her over onto her back. As he straddled her chest, her green eyes opened wide, her lovely lips parting in surprise.

Putting his hands lightly around her throat, he pushed his cock into her pretty mouth and closed his eyes. Ah, life was good.

Chapter 12

Kelsey sat cross-legged on the throw rug beside James' desk chair. She stared down at the legal pad on her lap, her pen poised, her mind blank. She knew what James expected—he'd read her enough of the endless, nauseating blogs written by brainwashed women and their deluded partners—but she couldn't seem to make her brain perform the necessary functions to get words onto the page.

At least her stomach was full, almost uncomfortably so. After the beating that morning Kelsey had fallen into a fitful sleep. James had woken her with a tray of food, and instead of the usual two or three bites, he'd let her eat the entire sandwich, plus a peach and a big glass of iced tea. Maybe the prick was feeling guilty.

Kelsey closed her eyes, trying to let go of the negative energy building inside her. It wasn't good to resist. It only made things worse. *Positive thoughts. Focus on the good things. Anger is destructive. He'll sense it and he'll punish you. James loves you. He takes care of you. This is your life now.*

She stole a glance at James. He was shirtless, wearing his favorite khaki shorts. His right hand was resting lightly over his crotch, his mouth hanging open, his eyes glued to the screen, though whether he was reading from one of his favorite blogs or staring at naked girls, Kelsey couldn't tell. At least he was leaving her alone, for the moment anyway.

Kelsey glanced down at the welt on her left breast. She could feel welts on her back, ass and thighs too, though she didn't dare shift her position to try and see, not with James right there beside her. She tried to recall what heinous crime she'd committed to deserve such brutal treatment. His words came back to her. *You forgot one of the prime rules of wifely submission. A wife doesn't voice what she does or does not want. She asks what would please her husband, and no more.*

Okay, so she'd fucked up. She'd forgotten the rules, but did that really merit the savage beating that had followed?

You were disobedient. Don't question him. Do what he says. You belong to him. To resist is to suffer. Focus on the good.

She knew she should listen to that voice of reason. James quite literally held her life in his hands. She knew better than to break the rules. Why was it suddenly so hard to control the rage she thought she'd conquered?

Because something was different now. Somehow that beating had reawakened a part of her that had been lying dormant during this time of forced captivity. She realized she'd been sinking deeper and deeper into a kind of trance, a self-induced pretense to make her lot bearable. How long until it was no longer pretense, but her reality? How long until she'd shut down completely, giving herself over to James' constant brainwashing and subjugation?

But was this sudden awareness any better? Stripped of her coping mechanism of denial and acceptance, she felt emotionally naked—shivering with rage, raw with pain and anger. *I don't belong to you,* she wanted to scream. *I belong to myself. I am my own person. I'm not your fucking obedient wife.*

"How's it going, Kelsey? You making progress? Let me see what you've written so far."

Kelsey jerked in startled surprise, the pen skittering over the page at the sound of James' voice. He held out his hand for the pad. Kelsey let out a deep, shuddering breath, willing her expression to go blank, terrified he'd see the rebellion on her face. Keeping her head down, reluctantly, Kelsey held out the pad.

James took it, his smile shifting to a frown as he read the only two sentences she'd managed to come up with so far. "That's it? That's all you wrote in twenty minutes?"

"I—I'm not used to writing with a pen. I think better with my fingers on a keyboard." That much was true. But James didn't trust her to get on his laptop. The internet was only a click away and she might blow the bastard's cover.

He might try to pretend that what they were doing was consensual, but he *had* to know better. Even he couldn't be that fucking deluded.

James read her words aloud, words he'd basically told her to write as an opening. "I am an obedient wife. My husband has been teaching me that to submit and obey are the hallmarks of a truly content and spiritual woman."

He handed the pad back to her. "It's not a bad start, but I know you can do better than that. Write about how good it makes you feel when you've pleased me. Write about why being punished makes you a better wife, and what steps you have been taking to make sure you keep your husband happy. Put some stuff in there about the sex, too. I want details about how intense your climaxes are within the framework of pleasing your husband. Tell about how grateful you are for the orgasms, but even more grateful for the opportunity to satisfy and serve your husband."

Why don't you write the fucking thing yourself?

Kelsey clapped her hand over her mouth, for half a heartbeat terrified she'd spoken those words aloud. James was watching her, a frown on his face. *Get a grip, get a grip,* Kelsey ordered herself. *Don't let him know anything's different. Don't let him think you've changed.*

She ordered her face to smooth itself into a bland smile, the expression he liked to call "serene". "Thank you, sir. Those are good suggestions." She picked up her pen and bent over the pad. She would use his words and make him happy so she could end this particular farce. What had he said? Something about punishment making her a better wife?

Fucking asshole. How does being brutalized, terrorized and half starved make me a better wife? And I'm not your fucking wife, anyway.

Kelsey realized she'd been writing, her hand moving of its own accord over the paper. She read what she had scrawled: I hate James. I hate James. I hate James.

With a gasp, she grabbed at the page and tore it from the pad, crumpling it into a ball. James looked down at her. "What? What's the problem?"

"Nothing." She hid the balled paper behind her back and pushed it beneath her bottom.

"Let me see. I bet it was fine. You need more confidence." He held out his hand. "Come on. Show me."

"No!" Oh god, why hadn't she crossed out those damning words? What was wrong with her? She couldn't let him see it. No, no, no, no.

James stood, towering over her. "Did you just say no to me?" His voice had taken on that silky, dangerous tone she knew meant trouble.

"Please. It's—it's just scribbles. Really. I'm starting over, see?" She held up the blank pad, her heart beating like a drum in her chest, the crumpled paper prickling beneath her still-tender ass.

James reached for her, gripping her forearms and hauling her to her feet. "To quote Shakespeare," he said with an ugly grin, "methinks the lady doth protest too much." He pulled her against him and wrapped one strong arm around her torso, while leaning down and grabbing the ball of paper with his other. He let her go and sat down, smoothing the page flat against his computer desk.

Kelsey sprinted away from him, not sure where she was going, but desperate to get there. Though mostly healed, the wound on her leg still slowed her gait, but fear spurred her forward. She ran through the living room to the kitchen and skidded to a stop in front of the silverware drawer. She yanked it open and groped for a sharp knife.

James came thundering into the room behind her. She whirled to face him, the knife clenched in her shaking fist. Blind with fear and fury, she raised the knife and rushed at him, aiming the point at his face.

She wanted to scare him.

She wanted to hurt him.

She wanted to kill him.

As she lunged, James lifted an arm to deflect her attack, while he reached for her with the other. The point of the knife slid along his shoulder, leaving a red line in its wake.

"You cut me!" James roared. "You fucking bitch, you cut me!" His hand closed over her wrist, squeezing and twisting until the agony of his grip forced her to let go.

The knife clattered to the floor.

She saw his fist hurtling toward her in the second before it made contact with her cheekbone, and then the floor slammed into her face.

~*~

James examined the wound in the mirror, his lips pressed into a grim line. The cut was deep and hurt like hell. He daubed gently at it with a damp cloth and applied some antibiotic cream.

It should heal okay without stitches, though it would probably leave a scar. His heart, however, would never heal from what had just happened. He stared down at the wrinkled piece of paper. The spiteful, cruel words hit him anew like a slap in the face each time he read them.

I hate James. I hate James. I hate James.

The hours, days and weeks of his constant, undying attention, of his firm but loving hand, and she had written those words! All her apparent strides in learning to embrace her life as an obedient, submissive and loving wife had been a fucking lie. She was still the same willful cunt she'd been before, just waiting for the chance to stab him in the heart, both literally and figuratively.

James went back into the bedroom. Kelsey was locked in the closet, where she would stay until he could calm himself down enough to deal with her. He felt bad for hitting her in the face like that. He'd been beside himself with pain and rage, but still, he knew his temper needed work. A responsible husband punished his wife, but never with anger.

He sat at the computer and logged onto the new site he'd discovered, a chat site for men who subscribed to the obedient wife lifestyle. Earl, the moderator and owner of the site, was online. James typed a direct message to Earl, a wise man with thirty years of experience in wife obedience training.

James: Hi Earl. Can we chat privately for a few minutes?

Earl: Sure. What's up, James?

James: I just had an incident with my wife. She was very disobedient.

Earl: Not good. What happened?

Did he tell Earl what Kelsey had actually done? As far as Earl knew, theirs was a consensual relationship. If he admitted the extent of what had happened, he might end up sharing more than was wise.

James: She was noncompliant with a writing assignment I gave her. When I rebuked her for it, she raised her hand to me. She struck me.

Earl: Raising your hand to your husband is a very serious infraction. A woman who does that clearly doesn't know her place. Not to be too harsh, James, but when a wife behaves like that, it's because the husband is too lax. You have failed in your teachings. She is not learning her lessons properly.

James: I put her in the punishment closet. I was afraid to do much else at this point, because I was acting out of anger. I know how important it is not to punish your wife in anger, but rather to wait until you are calm and rational.

Earl: That's certainly true. I admire your restraint. But remember that important adage about sparing the rod. Grave actions call for a grave response. She must learn that under no circumstances must she ever raise a hand to you. The lesson must be burned into her consciousness. I have found with my own wife that adding humiliation to the punishment makes for a more lasting impression.

James: How do you mean?

Earl: Well, not to put too fine a point on it, but some women, especially women who engage in our lifestyle, get a kind of thrill, sexual or otherwise, from corporal punishment. It becomes an almost erotic experience for them. But if you were to add a humiliation element, say, for example, if you were to take a video of her doing something private and post that video on our website for others to comment on, that might make more of an impact.

James felt his cock harden at the thought of displaying his woman for all the world to see. Prudence quickly intervened, however. Kelsey was officially a missing personal, after all.

James: We're kind of private that way. I wouldn't want to splash her face over the internet.

Earl: Who said anything about her face? Put a hood over her head. That could be part of her humiliation. It's dehumanizing. Make her do something normally kept private, something she wouldn't want the world to see.

James: Like masturbating?

Earl: Sure. Something like that, or maybe something even more private, like making her squat on newspaper to move her bowels while you film it. I have found just the threat of such a punishment *very* effective in keeping my wife in line.

James wasn't sure filming Kelsey taking a dump was the way he wanted to go, but he had to admit the idea of public humiliation was arousing. Still, there was the core issue still to deal with.

James: She said she hates me.

His face burned as he typed those words, and he was glad for the relative anonymity of the internet.

Earl: She doesn't mean it. If she's in this lifestyle, she wants your firm hand. She yearns for your control. She's just testing you, the way a child does. She's pushing the envelope. She's relying on you to put her in her place. It's where she longs to be. It's where she needs to be. It's up to you to put her back there so she feels cherished and safe.

James leaped on Earl's words, hope suddenly flaring where a moment before all had been dark. Maybe Earl was right! She had just been testing him. She *wanted* him to come down on her with a firm hand. She *needed* him to help her get to where she belonged. His mistake had been in being too easy on her. He needed to show her in no uncertain terms that he was in charge, no matter what she did. His love was unconditional, but so was his control.

Earl: You still there, James?

James: Yes. I was just mulling over what you said.

Earl: Let me know when you're ready. We'll do a public announcement on the site, and I'll send emails to all the members encouraging them to watch and comment. Your wife will think long and hard before she dares to raise her hand to you again. But James, don't forget one thing.

James: Yes?

Earl: Once she's been chastised, you must find it in your heart to forgive her, wholly and without reservation. That's the beauty of our kind of lifestyle. You punish her, but then you let it go, and the two of you can move forward with a clean slate. No lingering resentments, no recriminations. Just a purer love, made all the stronger by your firm hand and her repentant tears.

James: Thanks, Earl. I knew you'd have good advice. I'm feeling much better.

Earl: Glad to be of help. Don't dawdle now. You need to act fast, while the transgression is still fresh. Make the video now, punish her as you need to, and then let it go and move on.

James logged off, excited by what he was going to do. Earl was right—it was up to him to train Kelsey. If she still thought she hated him, it was because he wasn't doing a good enough job teaching her to accept her position as his obedient wife. He would do better, starting now.

He got a pillowcase from the linen closet, along with a hank of rope and a roll of duct tape. He placed the items on the edge of the bathtub and returned to the bedroom. He slid back the latch that kept the closet closed and pulled the door open.

Kelsey was lying on her side, curled into a fetal ball. She blinked as light flooded the small space. James saw the bruise that bloomed over her cheek like a purple flower, and his heart constricted with remorse, until he remembered the knife, and her murderous intent.

"Get up," he said brusquely. He reached for her, pulling her to her feet. She swayed as her eyes swept the long gash on his shoulder, her mouth falling open. "That's right," James said as he pulled her out of the closet. "You did that. You could have killed me. I hope you're proud of yourself."

"I'm sorry, James. I—"

"Save it. I don't want to hear it right now. Not a fucking word."

Wisely, she shut her mouth. He led her to the bathroom and pointed to the tub. "Get in and stay on your feet. We're going to make a movie."

She shrank back. "I said get in," James said, half-lifting her as he forced her into the bathtub. "This is what's called a humiliation exercise. Humiliation is an important tool, especially when training a disobedient willful wife such as yourself. Here's what's going to happen." As he talked, he pulled her hands behind her back and clipped her wrist cuffs together. "You're going to pee while standing up while I take a video of you. You're going to spread your legs and spread your cunt with your fingers so everyone can see you piss on yourself. Because I don't want to show your face on the internet, I'm going to put a hood over your head. And because I can't trust you to keep your mouth shut, I'm going to tape it shut."

"No, James. Please, this can't—"

"I said shut up!" James clenched his hand into a fist, aware he'd been about to strike her again. *Not in anger,* he reminded himself. *Not in anger.* He reached for the duct tape and pulled a strip from the roll. Putting one hand on the back of her neck to hold her still, he pressed the sticky tape over her mouth. Ignoring her muffled cries, he placed the pillowcase over her head and tied it in place around her neck with the rope.

His cock was rock hard as he drank in the sight of his naked girl with a hood over her head, her pretty breasts still sweetly welted from the morning whipping. "Spread your legs," he barked. "I know you must have to pee after all that tea you drank at lunch."

Reaching into his pocket, he pulled out his cell phone. "Go on. Show the world what a filthy little cunt you are. Piss for the camera, Kelsey." He hit the record button as he peered through the lens and said in a loud voice, "Wife, this is your punishment, and then all will be forgiven, as long as you promise to be a good girl from now on."

Kelsey stood still as stone for several long, defying moments. James paused the recording. "Do it, Kelsey. Or I'll tie you to the beam and whip you until you bleed. Is that what you want?"

He started the recording again. He would count to three. One… Two…

She reached with trembling hands for her pretty, smooth cunt, pulling the delicate lips apart as she spread her long, shapely legs. She stood that way for several seconds, and then a stream of golden urine splashed down, hitting the white porcelain with a satisfying splatter.

Again speaking for the camera, James said, "With this demeaning act, you have cleansed away your sins. Now we start over, you and I. A loving but firm husband and his obedient, willing wife."

Kelsey fell to her knees, and her shoulders began to shake. The poor darling was crying. James turned off the recording and slipped his phone into his pocket. He reached for the makeshift hood, quickly untying the rope and pulling it from Kelsey's head. "This will hurt a little, but I'll make it as fast as I can." He slipped his finger beneath an edge of the duct tape and ripped it quickly away.

He turned on the faucet and splashed it over Kelsey's legs and cunt, and then helped her to climb out of the tub. He pulled her into his arms. "All is forgiven, as I promised. After a stay in the punishment closet to contemplate your sins, we'll start with a clean slate. We will work extra hard, much harder than before, so I can help you learn your place as my obedient wife, my darling Kelsey. I won't give up on you, even if you've given up on yourself. Ours is a sacred bond and nothing, not even your childish anger, can break that bond."

James' cock was throbbing. Though he hadn't planned to, he found himself pushing Kelsey to the bath rug. He draped himself over her soft, lovely body, forced his thigh between her legs and guided his cock into her tight, silky perfection.

"I love you," he whispered. "No matter what."

Chapter 13

"Hold out your hands, palms up. I'm going to ask you a series of questions. If you answer incorrectly, I will chastise you. Don't feel bad if you mess up—it's part of the learning process. Once we're done with the lesson, as long as I see you've made the effort, you'll have something to eat."

At least she was out of the punishment closet. Kelsey wasn't sure how much time had passed since he'd forced her to pee in the tub. At least a day and a night, she thought, most of it spent curled in an uncomfortable ball on the floor of the pitch dark punishment closet. After the first several hours, she'd dared to knock on the door, begging to be let out, but James had ignored her. Eventually she gave up, worried she might be adding time to the punishment by speaking out. Surely he would have to let her out eventually.

She had slept fitfully off and on during the enforced captivity. At times she'd made herself stand up and move as much as she could in the small space to keep her muscles from cramping. After a while, though, she'd been too hungry and dizzy to bother.

She was kneeling now on the throw rug in the bedroom, glad at least to be in the light, though she felt hollow inside, aching with hunger and so very thirsty. James had set up the folding TV tray beside her, a plate of sliced apples, cheese and crackers taunting her, along with a big glass of iced tea.

She held out her hands as instructed. Her arms felt heavy, and she hoped this stupid lesson would be over quickly. Then she saw the birch switch in his hand. It was shorter than the one he sometimes used on her ass, but looked just as thin and whippy. James flicked it several times in the air, the whooshing sound a menacing promise. Kelsey's palms tingled and it took all her will not to drop her arms and wrap them protectively around herself.

Just answer correctly. You can do that. You know what he wants. Give it to him, and then you can eat and drink.

James hit his own palm lightly with the switch as he stared down at her. "Question number one. What are you?"

Okay, that was easy. He'd asked her that often enough. "An obedient wife."

The sudden cut of the switch across her left palm made Kelsey scream in both surprise and pain. Instinctively she brought her hand to her mouth, pressing it hard against her lips as she moaned.

"I chastised you because you forgot how to address me properly. Who am I?"

"Sir," Kelsey replied as she blinked back her tears. "I'm sorry, sir."

Damn it. She knew that! It was Obedience Wife Training 101. How had she forgotten?

James nodded. "I forgive you. I know you're hungry and aching. We'll start over. Back in position—palms up. Next time I chastise you, don't move out of position or I'll put you back in the closet. Now, what are you?"

"An obedient wife, sir." Kelsey looked down at her palms. The left one had an angry red line across it that throbbed and stung.

"Much better."

Concentrate. You can do this. Just get through it.

Kelsey's eyes slid toward the waiting food. She swallowed, waiting for the next question.

"When does an obedient wife speak?"

"When she's asked a direct question, sir."

"When your husband asks something of you that you find challenging, do you tell him you can't or won't do it?"

"No, sir."

"What is the proper response?"

"If it pleases you, sir, then it pleases me."

James nodded. "Very good." He paused, tapping the switch lightly against his thigh.

"Why do I keep you shaved?"

Kelsey bit her lip, trying to think. He shaved her underarms, legs and pussy every other day. She had to lie down on the bathroom floor and hold very still while he did it. Once he'd nicked her, and then he'd spanked her for causing him to do it, claiming she'd moved, though she hadn't. He was always rambling on about why he meted out this or that punishment, couching the abuse in terms of his obedient wife bullshit, but what was his specific rationale for the shaving?

She realized she'd just assumed he'd done it because he could—it was just one more way of exerting his power over her, and making her feel vulnerable. Was that the answer he wanted?

Think, think. What is it he's after? Say what he wants.

"Kelsey. Answer the question."

She blew out a breath. "Because it pleases you, sir?"

The switch cut across her right palm. She hissed her pain, though somehow managed to maintain her position.

"It does. But that's not why I do it. I've told you before. You must not have been paying attention." He struck her left palm again, the switch cutting across the initial welt. Kelsey howled in pain.

"Please, sir," she begged, "I can't do this. I can't think. I'm too hungry, too tired. The switch hurts too much."

"Stop it. You're acting like a child. Stop sniveling and whining. An obedient wife is honored to suffer at the hands of her husband. It teaches her she is cherished. Now, pay attention, because you're going to have to recite this rule until you get it right." He paused, and Kelsey struggled to control her whimpering so she could focus on his words.

"Are you listening?" James demanded.

"Yes, sir," she managed, her palms on fire with pain.

"The answer is twofold. You are shaved because an obedient wife must be completely accessible to her husband at all times. Female pubic hair is a direct affront to our lifestyle. I am the one to do the shaving because I exercise full but loving control over your body. My grooming you is a testament to my love for you. I care for you in all things. I support you, I feed you, I wash you, I claim your body, your heart and your soul. You belong to me. Now," James said ponderously, "why do I shave you?"

Fuck. How the hell am I supposed to remember all that? I'm hungry. I'm so hungry. Just get through it. The food is there. He means for you to have it. Just say what he said.

"Um, you shave me because an obedient wife must be accessible to her husband, sir." *What else? Shit, what else?* James raised the switch. "Your grooming is proof of your l-love." The word stuck in her throat. How could he call this love? She stumbled on, the apple and cheese waiting for her. "You care for me in all things. I belong to you, sir."

James pressed his lips together disapprovingly, but at least he didn't hit her again. "Better," he said grudgingly. "It's clear we still have work to do. I've been too easy on you, Kelsey. This is a new phase of training." He set down the switch and reached for his fly. Kelsey knew what was coming next. Her mouth was parched. She would do anything for a long drink of that iced tea.

"Thank me for the lesson, wife." James pulled out his cock, stroking it quickly to full erection.

"Thank you, sir," Kelsey managed. She opened her mouth to receive his cock, swaying on her knees as a sudden wave of dizziness rolled over her. The quicker she jerked him off, the sooner he would let her eat. He pushed his cock into her mouth and gripped her head between his hands. As usual after a punishment session, he came quickly, his cock lodged so far back in her throat that she didn't even need to swallow.

He held her that way for several long seconds before finally letting her go. He tucked himself back into his shorts and bent down, lifting her into his arms.

"Hungry, sweetheart?" he murmured as he laid her gently on the bed.

"Yes, sir," she breathed. She'd made it through the ordeal. Now he would be kind to her, at least for a while.

The bed was so soft, the sheets cool against her skin. She waited as James moved the food tray closer. The first bite of apple was like heaven against her tongue. It was followed by a long drink of the tea and then a cube of sharp, tangy cheese. He let her eat everything on the plate, and she found herself almost grateful, even though all that food at once made her tummy hurt.

She lay back against the pillows, nearly content. She longed to close her eyes and slip into dreams, but James said, "I want to show you something."

He brought the laptop to the bed. Kelsey again found herself grateful—he was allowing her to rest on the soft, comfortable bed, instead of making her kneel or stand beside his computer desk as he usually did. He tapped the keyboard and then turned the laptop so she could see the screen.

"My posting made quite a stir on the *Control Your Wife* site. Your punishment in the bathtub was a good lesson for other errant wives, apparently. I got lots of positive feedback."

Kelsey shrank back against the pillows and closed her eyes. The experience in the tub had been at once humiliating and terrifying. She didn't want to relive it by being forced to watch, but then, he wasn't asking her what she wanted.

If it pleases you, sir, then it pleases me.

If only she could actually believe that. As James had told her so often, if only she could get to a place of acceptance, this would all be so much easier.

To accept is to give up. Never give up!

The voice that had once been a rallying cry inside her head was now barely a whisper. It was so hard to keep on fighting. And to what purpose? All it got her was punishment and pain.

James clicked on the video and it began to play. Kelsey realized she hadn't really looked at herself since James had abducted her. Even when in front of the bathroom mirror she had averted her eyes, not wanting to see what she had become. Now she stared at the too-thin naked girl with a pillowcase over her head and welts clearly visible on her breasts and thighs.

"Wife," boomed a voice from the computer's speaker—James' voice, but deeper somehow, more resonant. "This is your punishment, and then all will be forgiven, as long as you promise to be a good girl from now on."

A good girl? Was that all he wanted? She tried to be a good girl, but she never got it right. Did the other so-called obedient wives get it right? Were they constantly punished for the slightest infraction? Were they beaten, starved and humiliated as she was, all in the name of love?

It was too much to handle—too much to bear. She was exhausted, she was weak, she couldn't fight any longer. She felt as if she were standing on the edge of a cliff, her toes curled around crumbling stone and dirt as she struggled to hang on to what was left of her sanity and her will.

Kelsey watched the girl in the video reach with shaking hands to spread her denuded sex, and then the gush of urine splashing down between her legs. She felt a hot burn of humiliation spreading over her chest, throat and cheeks but she didn't dare to look away from the screen. As the tortured girl sank to her knees in the video, tears blurred Kelsey's vision.

I can't do this. Not anymore.

I'm done.

The unfolding horror on the computer screen was like a shove against her bare back, and she found herself tumbling into the abyss, her mind folding in upon itself. She heard a low, anguished cry and realized it was her own voice she was hearing. She felt the sobs surge up through her body, deep, wracking sobs that shook her frame and forced her mouth into an open howl.

Strong arms enfolded her, wrapping her in a tight, warm embrace. "That's it, sweetheart," James crooned softly in her ear. "Let it all out. With your tears, you're releasing all the evil, willful toxins that keep you from truly submitting. Cry, baby. Cry it all out. Give yourself over to the tears."

She let go of the last vestige of control, releasing a rush of tears, a torrent of sorrow, a flood of surrender. She cried until her throat was raw, her mind empty, her body spent. She cried until her heart melted beneath the barrage of tears. She cried until there was nothing left.

The darkness that moved over her soul was a kind of welcome oblivion, a sort of exhausted peace. As she lay drifting, she felt herself being rocked and the steady, rhythmic movement was soothing. She was cocooned and warm in strong, supportive arms.

"Sleep, darling. You're safe now."

She was safe. Safe in his arms. Why had she resisted for so long? She had moved through fire and darkness, and emerged at last in a peaceful place, as vast as the ocean. It was such a relief to let go at last and she felt herself sink like a stone into the silence.

~*~

Earl: Hey there, James. Got another video for me?

James: Actually, I wanted to get your advice.

Earl: Sure, what's up?

James: Is it possible to go too far with obedience training?

Earl: How do you mean?

James: Well, I know the video was well-received, but when I had my wife watch it, she got kind of weird. I mean, it was almost like she went into a kind of shock. It's been nearly a week and she still doesn't seem to have really recovered from it.

Earl: You're probably overreacting. Is she still behaving?

James: Yes.

Earl: Then I wouldn't worry about it too much. Don't be so hard on yourself.

James: I don't know. I'm wondering if maybe I was too hard on her.

Earl: Don't be ridiculous. That video was gold. The hits on the site have gone through the roof since you posted it. Several very lucrative monetizing opportunities are coming my way as a result. And I have you to thank, James. In fact, I was thinking of approaching you about a weekly, or even a daily video. Your wife was made for the camera.

James: I'm confused. I thought this was a member's only site for people committed to the lifestyle?

Earl: Sure, sure, it is, of course. But it doesn't run itself, you know. You don't begrudge me trying to make some money to keep the site going, do you? We all do our part in the community, after all. I'm thinking you could record your daily training sessions, and we could follow your wife's development as she blossoms into a fully submissive obedient wife. You could take us deeper—show us all aspects of training and service, including the sexual, if you get my drift. Depending on your comfort level, of course. I mean, no pressure or anything, but we might be talking some serious cash here, my friend. I'm willing to do a fifty-fifty split.

James frowned at the screen. What the fuck was Earl going on about? Here he'd come to trust the man as a kind of mentor and advisor in the lifestyle, and he was coming across as some kind of opportunistic creep looking for amateur porn. What the hell?

James: I'll get back to you on that. Gotta go. TTYL.

He logged off the site, angry with both Earl and himself. That's what came of opening up to others. He should have known better. He did know better. He didn't need Earl's advice or permission. He'd learned all he needed from others. He and Kelsey were happiest when it was just the two of them. They didn't need anyone else.

If he'd gone too far with Kelsey, it had been for her own good. He'd had to break her down in order to rebuild her into an obedient wife. It was the price they both had to pay.

He closed the laptop with resolve and strode from the bedroom. He found Kelsey in the kitchen on her hands and knees, scrub brush in hand. He watched her from the doorway as she washed the floor. He liked her to do it that way, instead of using a mop. He especially liked to stand behind her while she was doing it, so he could watch her ass sway as she worked. It always got him hard, and this time was no exception.

"Get up and bend over the sink," he ordered. Kelsey turned toward him with a small gasp, a startled look on her face. She often seemed lost in her own world lately.

"Go on," he snapped impatiently. "You heard me. That hesitation will cost you. You'll have to be punished for that." James' cock throbbed at the thought. She'd been giving him less and less cause to punish her lately, and he sometimes found himself creating obstacles for her just so she would fail. He knew that wasn't really fair, but hey, he made the rules, right? His word was law.

Kelsey dropped the scrub brush into the bucket of soapy water and scrambled to her feet. She moved quickly to the sink and bent over it. James let his shorts fall to the linoleum as he moved toward her. He kicked her legs wider apart and gripped her hips, his cock tingling as it nudged along the cleft of her ass.

He grabbed one of the many tubes of lubricant he now kept around the cabin so he'd have them whenever he needed them. He'd found himself increasingly drawn to anal sex. There was something so powerful about taking her that way, and he loved the way she cried out when he rammed himself inside her tight passage.

He squirted a blob of lube onto the head of his cock and stroked the pucker between her ass cheeks with his fingertips. He felt her tense. "You resist me," he told her. "You've become such an obedient girl, but in this one area you still resist. I'll have to punish you for that too, you know that, right?"

"Yes, sir."

He pushed the head of his cock into her tight little ass. Kelsey squealed.

"Why do I punish you, Kelsey?" He gripped her hips and pushed deeper.

"Because you love and cherish me, sir," Kelsey gasped prettily.

James rammed his cock deep inside her. Kelsey was panting. He reached around her and shoved a finger into her cunt. "Go on," he urged. "Why do you need to be punished?"

"Punishment purifies me, sir. It teaches me. It helps make me worthy to be your wife, sir."

"That's right." He began to thrust inside her tiny hole. Christ, it felt so fucking good. When he was done, he'd suspend her from the beam and whip her until he drew blood. Not only because she needed it, but because he wanted it.

The realization at once thrilled and frightened him. Sometimes he woke at night in a cold sweat, wondering what the hell he had become. What had happened to his innocent dreams of wedded bliss? When had he slipped into this bizarre role of lord and master over another human being?

It's only to teach her, he reassured himself as he moved in her tight grip. *She needs to be controlled. She is happy and at peace. You had to break her to build her up again. It was the only way. It is the only way.*

He closed his eyes, imagining his beloved suspended by rope from the ceiling beam, her naked, bare body crisscrossed with welts, both the new ones he would paint on her with the whip and the switch, and the fading ones from her daily lessons and punishments. His balls tightened as a powerful orgasm coiled inside him, making his body rigid in the seconds before it exploded through his shaft.

"Yes!" he cried. "Yes!"

He leaned heavily against Kelsey as he recovered himself. Finally he pulled away from her and stepped back. She turned slowly and sank gracefully to his feet. "Thank you, sir," she murmured, looking up at him with eyes as empty and vacant as green glass.

Chapter 14

James pulled the ropes from the ceiling beam and coiled them neatly into a pile. He stared around the cabin, thinking about the months the two of them had shared together here. He would miss the particular solitude of this place, but it was also exciting to contemplate a new beginning, one without any memories of his punitive father glaring across his paper at the breakfast table, or his tittering, anxious mother offering subtle criticism cloaked in a guise of concern.

He placed the rope in the large duffel that contained the various implements and objects he used to control and train his obedient wife, and, in spite of himself, he felt his cock harden in his jeans. He hadn't whipped Kelsey to bleeding in some time. Though he knew it was wrong, he couldn't deny the fierce, dark thrill he got every time he drew her blood. He loved to plunge his cock into her ass afterward, her skin on fire, her sweet, breathy cries urging him on.

Idly stroking his erection, he went to the safe his father had installed in the kitchen pantry when the cabin was first built, and removed the large lockbox that contained most of his inherited fortune. Ironic that the parents of a banker had never believed in banks, and had hoarded and saved the bulk of their money in hidden safes in their various homes, most of it converted to gold bullion and coins. Lucky, too, that James had continued the tradition with his share of the wealth once they'd died. There would be no sudden withdrawals of substantial, reportable income. He would be able to disappear without a trace, just as Kelsey Rowan had done four months before.

The box was too heavy to set on the table, so he placed it on the floor beside the couch, straining from the effort. He retrieved the key from its hiding place in the fake panel of the wall behind the couch. As he unlocked the box and stared at the neatly stacked rows of gold bars, gold coins, precious gemstones and hundred dollar bills, he went through his plans once more in his head. His house back in the city was listed with the broker, and this cabin would be listed as well, come spring. He would email the broker with a PO Box, once he and Kelsey got settled across the border.

He removed the folder he'd recently placed in the box and opened it to examine the new passport he'd had made, the one belonging to *Amelia Bennett,* with a photo of Kelsey beside the name. He'd paid quite a bit for it online, but it looked identical to his own and matched the driver's license he'd had made for her in case any additional identification was needed. He replaced the passports and picked up the small blue velvet box, balancing it on the palm of his hand.

He could hear the water running in the bathroom and wondered how Kelsey was getting on with her chore of washing the base of the toilet and the floor around it with an old toothbrush. He did enjoy having her stand at attention while he completed his inspection. Try as she might, he always found room for improvement, which led, of course, to a necessary punishment before he sent her back to try the task again.

He walked into the bedroom, the velvet box still in his hand. He watched Kelsey on her knees from the door of the bathroom, her ass facing him, the bare lips of her sweet, pink cunt peeking between her legs as she moved.

"Kelsey."

She jerked at the sound and he heard her sudden intake of breath. Remaining on her hands and knees, she turned her head. "Yes, sir?"

She looked so beautiful, her luxuriant coppery hair cascading in a tumble around her face, her eyes large and luminous beneath sharply etched cheekbones, her small, perfect breasts tipped with dark pink nipples that made his mouth water. If her expression was more empty than alive, she more than made up for it with her obedience and sexual responsiveness. And once he got her down to Mexico, things would be different, he was sure of it.

Though he'd planned his surprise for after dinner, suddenly James couldn't wait another second.

"Get up," he said. "I have something for you." He led her to the throw rug in the center of the bedroom where he usually had her kneel, but when she started to sink to her knees, he stopped her with a smile. "No," he said, "you stand. This time I'm the one to go on bended knee."

He knelt awkwardly on one knee and held up the blue velvet jewelry box while Kelsey stared down in surprise. For the first time since he'd claimed her all those months ago, he felt the kind of boyish nervousness he used to experience at the bank when he talked to her, his heart filled with unrequited longing. He smiled to hide the feeling and opened the box.

Kelsey stared down at the contents—matching wedding rings of twenty-four carat rose gold. James lifted out the smaller ring and reached for Kelsey's left hand. He took a breath and launched into the speech he'd been practicing in his head ever since he'd purchased the rings several days before.

"These rings," he said, "are symbols of the endless circle of our love. With this ring, you are bound to me for eternity in obedience and submission." He pushed the ring onto her finger, and then took the second ring, placing it in her hand.

"Go on," he urged, trying not to let his irritation enter his voice as she just stood there, a blank expression on her face. She wasn't used to taking action on her own anymore. That odd, vacant look he hated had entered her eyes. He decided to ignore it. He wouldn't let her ruin this moment. "Put it on my finger," he said, his voice coming out more brusquely than he'd intended.

She did as she was told, slipping the gold band into place. It felt cold and heavy against his skin. James continued his speech. "With this ring, you acknowledge me as your husband, your lord and master, who will cherish and love you all the days of your life."

Kelsey said nothing.

James wanted to slap her. Instead he stood and took her arm, pulling her into the living room. She just didn't understand yet, that was all. She'd used to be so intelligent, he recalled suddenly, back when he'd first fallen for her. It was one of the things he'd admired about her. She wasn't only beautiful, she was bright, and quick to laugh—a deep, throaty laugh that made others laugh with her.

When was the last time he'd heard her laugh, or seen her smile? Where was the spark that used to light up those lovely green eyes? James frowned— these thoughts weren't productive, and he pushed them away. He would make her eyes sparkle with what he had to show her next.

He let her go and strode toward the lockbox. He turned to her—she was standing where he'd left her, arms hanging limply at her sides. "Come over here," he said. She approached and knelt in front of him, eyes downcast.

"I want to show you something." James lifted the lid and tilted the box so Kelsey could see the contents. She stared at it, her face coming alive at last as she took in what was there.

"There's enough there to take care of us for the rest of our lives, especially down in Mexico." James couldn't keep the pride and excitement from his voice. "We're going to buy a little villa down in some out of the way place where no one will interfere in our business. Once we're settled, we can start our family."

He hadn't asked her a direct question, but Kelsey opened her mouth anyway. "A family?" she said in a faint voice, her face suddenly drained of color.

James nodded eagerly. "Yes. That's why I stopped your birth control last week. Didn't you notice? We're going to make a baby, you and me. We'll have lots of children. I'll teach them to be good and obedient too. You will be their example. I know you'll make me proud."

Color had started to seep back, rising in a flush over her neck and reaching her cheeks. "A family?" she said again, this time louder, as if the words were a curse instead of a blessing. Something was changing in her face as she stared at him, her eyes sparking suddenly like green fire, her mouth twisting into an ugly frown.

"Children? Babies?" she demanded incredulously. "You're going to do to them what you've done to me? You would beat them and starve them and terrify them into submission?"

James gaped at her, too stunned to respond. He could feel the heat coming into his face as rage began its slow rumble inside him.

She would pay for this. Oh god, she would pay.

Kelsey jumped up, her face a mask of fury. "No," she dared to say. And then again. "No. No, no, no, no, no, no, no!" Her voice rose with each word, hysteria lifting it higher and higher. James felt his anger deepen with each repetition, and still she would not stop.

He reached to take his ungrateful babbling bitch of a wife in hand, but before he could act, she sprinted away from him, heading in the direction of the kitchen. He took off after her, easily catching her. He fell upon her, sending her crashing to the floor beneath him.

He got to his feet and hauled her upright. Picking her up, he threw her over his shoulder and carried her into the bedroom. Though he'd packed the beam ropes, the chains were still in place on the headboard of the bed. He threw her face down on the mattress and grabbed her wrists, quickly forcing them into the cuffs and then wrenching the chain tight to pull her arms taut.

Don't punish in anger, a small voice insisted in his head, but his fury soon drowned it out. He'd been so certain she'd be thrilled with the rings and his plans. Her outright rejection was like a stinging slap in the face. *She never loved you, you idiot,* that annoying voice persisted. *You stole her love, you hold her through fear. You have to stop this. You can't go on.*

Pain and fury thumped through his veins and beat in his ears like a drum drowning out that annoying, niggling voice. Kelsey was struggling in the chains, something she hadn't done in months, and she was still chanting that infuriating single-word mantra—*no, no, no, no, no, no!* A proper obedient wife *never* said no to her husband. She had to be punished! She would never respect him if he let her get away with this flagrant disobedience.

He struck her bottom with his bare hand, needing to feel skin on skin. He hit her hard, as hard as he'd ever hit her, his palm landing with such force that it pushed her into the mattress. Kelsey howled with each blow, but at least she was no longer saying *no*. He hit her again and again and again, until his hand was stinging, his wrist aching. He hit her until his palm was numb. He hit her until her struggling ceased, and her cries had quieted to hoarse whimpers.

Finally he dropped his hand, startled to realize his own face was covered with tears. He reached for Kelsey's cuffed wrists and released them. Gathering her into his arms, he carried her to the punishment closet and dumped her inside. "I'll let you out when you're ready to apologize," he informed her. "You'll need to ask me to please let you out, and tell me you're sorry for being such a very, very naughty girl."

She didn't respond.

Angrily, James shut the closet door and slid the latch into place. Once he got her down to Mexico he would step up the training. The word *no* would be erased completely from her vocabulary. He would begin again, breaking her down once more so he could build her back into the girl of his dreams. Angrily, he wiped the tears from his eyes.

They would leave first thing in the morning.

James hadn't slept much the night before, all too aware of Kelsey still in the closet. He'd heard her whimpering during the night and had kept waiting for her to ask to be let out, but she never had. He must have finally drifted to sleep around dawn, and now it was later than he'd planned, the sun already up and streaming into the bedroom window.

He got out of bed and showered. He would finish packing the car, and then he'd let Kelsey out of the closet even if she hadn't asked by then. He was just pulling on his clothing when he heard the sound of car tires crunching up the gravel drive.

With an anxious glance at the closet, he hurried out of the bedroom, pulling the door closed behind him. He walked quickly into the living room and peered through the window that looked out on to the front porch.

A tall man with broad shoulders was climbing out of a red car, his blond hair glinting in the autumn sunlight. He didn't look like a cop, and anyway, they always seemed to travel in pairs, but just the same, James wasn't taking any chances. He hurried to the door and pulled it open, stepping out onto the porch as he pulled the cabin door closed behind him.

The man appeared to be in his late twenties or early thirties. Maybe he was just some damn salesman. James would get rid of him and then finish packing the car. He moved to the screen door as the man climbed the steps.

"Yes? Can I help you?" James said, crossing his arms over his chest.

"James Bennett?"

James' sense of disquiet deepened, but he kept his face neutral. "Who wants to know?"

The man slipped his hand into his jacket and held out a business card. "My name is Michael Johansen. I'm a private investigator. May I come in?"

James stepped back abruptly from the screen door. "I'm sorry, what?" he said inanely.

"I won't take much of your time." He peered through the screen with intense blue eyes that made James uncomfortable. "Someone's life might literally depend on it," the man continued in a deep voice. "Just a few questions and I'll be on my way."

"I'm awfully busy," James said. "I'm packing up. The house is a mess—"

"We can talk right here, then." The man squared his shoulders with determination.

James unlatched the screen door. He would answer the guy's questions and send him on his way. The cops had closed the case on Kelsey. Maybe this guy was nosing around about something entirely different. But he had known who James was...

James stepped back as the man came onto the porch. Without invitation, the man sat on one of the porch chairs. James remained standing, his arms crossed. "What's this all about?" he demanded.

The man pulled out a small notebook and extracted a photo from it. He held it out for James' inspection. James took the photo, relieved to see his hand was steady. His heart was suddenly thumping high in his throat. Kelsey stared back at him—not the thin waif of a girl she'd become, but a younger, more robust version, grinning broadly for the camera.

"Kelsey," he breathed before he realized he'd uttered a sound. He sank into a chair, unable to look away from the image.

"That's right," the big man said. "Kelsey Rowan. You used to work together?"

James met the guy's intense gaze, willing himself to be calm. The man knew nothing. He was just fishing. Who the fuck hired him? He forced himself to hand the photo back to the man.

"Yes. I know she's been missing for a while." James hoped his expression conveyed the right amount of concern, without being overly anxious. "I thought the police had stopped the investigation. Who are you working for?"

"The police may be less focused on the case right now, but the file is still active. I'm working for Kelsey's parents. There are some new leads. Promising leads."

James sat straighter in the chair and pulled his lips into something approximating a smile. "That's good news," he forced himself to say. "So what do you want from me? I've been away from the bank for months."

"So I understand. Cancer, is it?" His gaze was skeptical and James wanted to smack him.

"That's right. I'm in remission, but thanks for asking."

"I spoke with your colleagues at the bank. There was a young woman, Jenny Murphy, remember her?

"Of course I remember her," James snapped. "She was on my team." A chubby girl, James recalled, never especially pleasant, though she did her job. She and Kelsey had lunch together a lot, mostly at the park.

"She, uh" — the man glanced down at his small notebook and looked up again — "she noted that you seemed to be especially interested in Kelsey. You had Kelsey sit directly across from your desk and Jenny noticed you were often, uh, watching her?"

That fucking cunt.

James forced a small laugh. "I'm sorry, I don't know what you mean. Kelsey was a relatively new employee. I had Mark Hammond shift desks so Kelsey could be near her supervisor, in case she had questions or concerns. As to *watching* Kelsey, I have no idea what Jenny is talking about."

He leaned forward, offering a conspiratorial smile. "Jenny was, you know, a little heavy, in her late twenties and single, a little desperate, perhaps. She might have resented all the attention a pretty young woman, the new girl, if you will, got from the guys in the department."

The investigator stared at James for a moment and then slowly nodded. "Yes, all right. I see." He scribbled something in his little notebook, and James wanted to grab the thing and hurl it across the porch.

Instead, he started to rise from his chair. "Sorry I can't help you. Now if there's nothing—"

The investigator made no move to rise. "I see you're wearing a wedding ring. I didn't know you had married." The man lifted his eyebrows in question.

James covered his hand, his fingers closing over the ring. He felt himself flushing. "I'm sorry," he said stiffly. "I wasn't aware my marital status was any of your business."

"You said you were packing?" the man continued, not missing a beat.

"Yes. Yes, I'm—I'm going on a trip."

"With your wife?"

James stood. "We're done here, Mr. Johnson, or whatever your name is. Unless you have a warrant or something—"

The man stood as well. "A warrant?" he said musingly. "Think I need one?"

"This is private property," James said angrily. He took a step toward the man.

"No problem. I'll just stop by later. Maybe chat with your wife—"

"Yeah, okay. You do that. Come by this afternoon." *We'll be long gone, you son of a bitch.*

"All right then." The man extended a big hand and James had no choice but to take it. He watched as the man got into his car, waiting by the screen door until the bastard drove out of sight.

His heart was still beating too fast, and he felt like he was going to throw up. He sank into the porch chair and saw that, along with his business card, the man had left the snapshot of Kelsey. James reached for it and stared down at the image. It wasn't one he'd seen before. She was probably in her late teens in the shot, perhaps on a family vacation. The picture captured just her head and shoulders, though from the thin blue straps on her sun-burnt shoulders, he guessed she was wearing a bathing suit. Her face was tan, the apples of her cheek pink, her thick auburn hair tousled and windblown, her lovely green eyes glowing with happiness.

Again he found himself wondering when he had last heard her joyous, full-throated laugh, or seen her smile. When had the color faded from her cheeks, and the sparkle from her eyes? Where had the happy, sassy, funny girl he used to know and admire disappeared to?

She's gone, that small, cold voice inside his head replied. *You killed her.*

Tears splattered down onto the photo of the lost girl. James felt something crack inside his heart, the pieces shattering like shards of cold, sharp glass in his chest. He dropped his head into his hands with an anguished cry as Kelsey's smiling image fell silently to the floor.

Chapter 15

Kelsey heard the soft metallic sound of the closet latch sliding back and she opened her eyes. She knew she was expected to lift herself into a kneeling position, hands resting on her knees, head bowed in wifely submission, but she only curled tighter into herself.

The fog that had surrounded her all these months had been burned away with James' horrifying pronouncement that they would be starting a family. It was as if she'd been blinded by James' constant reign of terror, but now, suddenly, she could see again, and there was no going back. There was no way she could return to that quiet but dark and dangerous place, even if her life depended on it. Other potential lives now hung in the balance. She would rather die than go along with his monstrous plans.

Earlier she had heard James stomping around, pulling drawers open and slamming them closed. No doubt he expected her to beg to be let out, but she wasn't going to beg for anything—not anymore. She lay on the hard wood in silence, waiting for the closet door to open, steeling herself for the next onslaught of abuse.

Seconds ticked by, turning into minutes. Why had he unlocked the door if he didn't plan to let her out?

Finally, Kelsey sat up, wincing as her sore bottom brushed the hard closet floor. How long had he left her there this time? She was hungry, but then, she was always hungry. It had definitely been overnight, judging by the pressure in her bladder.

What the hell was taking James so long to open the fucking door? She really had to pee. Her bladder was aching, and the prospect of being let out made it that much worse as she imagined the relief she would feel when she sat on the toilet.

Hurry up, you bastard.

She thought she heard the sound of the front door clicking shut, and then the rumble of a car engine, which faded slowly away. What was going on?

"James?" she ventured finally.

Nothing.

She moved in the dark, feeling for the door, closing her hand over the knob. Did she dare?

She turned it slowly, her heart beating fast. Was he standing on the other side, waiting for just such impertinence? Was he watching the knob turn? Was this just another trap?

She dropped her hand, her courage momentarily failing her. What game was he playing?

Finally, her bladder spurring her on, she reached for the knob again, listening hard for the slightest sound. All she could hear was the beating of her own heart, an insistent *boom, boom, boom* in her chest.

Slowly, slowly, she pushed at the door, freezing for a moment as the hinges creaked, the sound sharp as a knife. "James?" she called softly.

Nothing.

She pushed the door wider, her ears pricked. She squinted against the sudden light that assailed her, blinking rapidly as her eyes adjusted to the glare. The sun was shining brightly through the bedroom window, its angle telling her it was late morning.

Where was James?

Her eyes swept the room. It was empty, everything packed. "James?" she called again, louder this time. If he was there, she'd just as soon face him, damn it. She crawled into the room and pushed herself slowly to her feet. He must have wanted her to come out of the closet, she reasoned, or why had he unlatched it? Again she pondered what game he was playing. How was she supposed to figure out the rules?

Her bladder directed her next moves, and she half-danced, half skipped toward the bathroom, clutching at herself the way a child might as she made her way to the toilet. She sighed with relief as she peed, voiding as quickly as she could, certain James would appear at any second.

She finished and wiped herself. Flushing, she jumped up from the toilet and went to the sink, avoiding her image as she always did as she splashed water on her face and reached for a towel. Then, though she knew she shouldn't, she turned around and twisted back to see the damage from the spanking. Her bottom was mottled with dark red and purple bruises and she winced at the sight.

Don't forget it, she told herself. *Don't float away again. Stay conscious. Stay focused. Fight!*

Resolved, she turned away from the image and ventured back into the bedroom, still not sure how she would react when she saw him. Should she try to play his game? Should she drop to her knees, beg his forgiveness and promise to be a good girl?

I can't. I can't do it. Not again. I won't.

Steeling herself, she entered the living room, girding herself to face her tormentor.

The room was empty.

She walked into the kitchen, her heart beating so fast she thought she might pass out.

He wasn't there.

She opened a drawer, looking for something sharp to use as a weapon. James had kept the knives hidden ever since she'd slashed him all those months ago. But a fork would work too. She could stab it into his eye, and then make a run for it.

She grabbed a fork and returned to the living room. She peered through the front window. She couldn't see his car, but that didn't necessarily mean it wasn't there.

She ran into the bedroom and yanked open a drawer, searching for something to wear. The drawers were empty. She went into the bathroom and rummaged in the linen closet, pulling down one of James' old T-shirts that she used as a rag when cleaning. It was better than nothing, and she pulled it over her head. In the mudroom she found an old pair of flip flops, and she slid her feet into them. There was a jacket hanging on the peg, and she put this on as well. She would make her way to the main road and flag someone down.

Then she heard it—the sound of a car pulling up to the house. He was back. She had to get out! But how? There was only one door to the cabin, and he was right outside.

She heard the car door open and slam, and then heavy footsteps moving inexorably toward the screen door. She heard it swing open.

Grabbing the fork, she raced to the wall beside the door. She would leap from behind the open door and catch him unaware. She would stab him in the face. She would kick him as hard as she could in the balls and then make a run for it.

The door opened, hiding her for the moment behind it. She could hear him walking into the room.

She counted to three as she gathered her courage. With the fork clutched in her fist, she pushed the door and leaped out from behind it.

"Hello? Anyone home?"

Kelsey froze in confusion, the fork falling from her hand to the floor. Acting off pure instinct, she lunged headlong into the intruder's massive chest.

She fell heavily on top of someone who wasn't James as the two of them hit the floor. The man was bigger, burlier, his hair a dark blond, his eyes a brilliant blue. He sat up and then hoisted himself upright, lifting Kelsey as he stood.

"Sorry I startled you. You okay?" he said as he took a step back. Then he peered at her, his eyes widening. "Oh my god," he said softly. "You're Kelsey, aren't you? Kelsey Rowan. You're skin and bones. And those bruises and welts…" His face crumpled with pity. "Jesus Christ, what did that bastard do to you?"

Kelsey stared back at the man, her mouth working, though no sound issued. The world tilted as her knees buckled beneath her. Strong arms caught her as she fell and then the world went black.

When Kelsey opened her eyes, at first she had no idea where she was, or what was happening. As she came more to herself, she realized she was in the living room, lying on the sofa. She sat up abruptly, pushing through the wave of dizziness that assailed her. James would punish her if he found her on the furniture without permission. She started to roll to the ground when a deep voice that was not James' stopped her.

"Hey there. You passed out for a minute. I was getting worried. I was about to call 9-1-1." The blond man she'd barreled into was sitting on the chair catty-corner to the sofa. "You okay?"

Kelsey nodded, though she wasn't sure if she was or not.

"I'm really sorry I scared you so bad," the stranger continued. "I had to come back, though. I didn't buy Bennett's story, but he pretty much threw me off the premises. It suddenly occurred to me that he said come to back this afternoon because he didn't plan on being here. When I saw that his car was gone, I was afraid I'd come too late. My god, if I'd known *you* were here, right here in the cabin, I would have knocked him out cold and broken the door down."

"What's happening?" Kelsey said, her mind still moving slowly. "Where's James? Who are you?" She wrapped her arms around her torso, glad she was at least wearing the T-shirt and jacket, but keenly aware of her nakedness beneath it. She tucked her legs underneath her body and looked at the man.

He started to extend his hand, apparently thought better of it and dropped it into his lap. "I'm Michael

Johansen. I'm a private investigator. Your parents hired me to find you. I've been on the case for a week or so. Something about Bennett just didn't sit right with me, especially after I talked to him this morning."

"This morning?" Kelsey echoed. "You were here this morning?"

"Yeah." Michael shook his head. "He told me I could come back this afternoon to talk to his wife. If I'd known you were here all along, oh my god..."

Kelsey brought her hands together and stared down at the offending band of gold still on her finger. Twisting it, she yanked it off and hurled it with all her might against the wall. She saw that Michael was staring at her and she started to laugh, a bubble of hysteria bursting from her lips.

"His wife," she gasped, "his obedient, submissive wife!" She doubled over, laughing so hard she could barely catch her breath, the sound echoing like a howl in her ears. She wasn't sure when the laughing segued into sobbing, but all at once the tears were streaming down her cheeks, and Michael had wrapped his arms around her and was holding her in a gentle but firm embrace.

"What did he do to you?" Michael murmured as he held her. "What did that bastard do to you?"

Eventually Kelsey quieted. She liked being held in this man's arms. He was so different from James, and he smelled good, like wood smoke and peppermint. She felt safe for the first time in a hundred years, a hundred lifetimes.

Finally Michael let her go, settling her gently against the back of the sofa. "I'm going to call your parents, okay? Let them know I've found you. Then we should call the cops. Do you have any idea where Bennett went? Do you think he's coming back?"

"Mexico," Kelsey said. "We were supposed to go to Mexico this morning, but when he unlatched the punishment closet—"

"The punishment closet?" Michael repeated, his face darkening with anger. "We have to get this bastard, Kelsey. He won't get away with what he's done to you."

Kelsey nodded her agreement. Then she saw the lockbox on the floor beside the sofa. "Oh," she said, confused and then afraid. He wouldn't have left the lockbox full of gold and cash if he weren't planning to return. She realized she'd been hoping against hope that he was well and truly gone.

"What?" Michael said as he followed her gaze. He stood and moved around the sofa to see what she was looking at. "What's this?"

The key was still in the lock. Michael crouched beside it and lifted the lid. "Whoa," he breathed. "What the hell...? There's a fortune in this thing,

Kelsey." He turned and stared at her with those penetrating blue eyes. "Where in the hell did he get all this? Did he rob a bank or something?"

Kelsey shook her head. "It's his inheritance, he said. He showed it to me last night."

Michael lifted something from the lockbox and held it out toward her. "Maybe this letter will shed some light. It's addressed to you."

Kelsey saw the envelope with her name written on the front in James' angular hand. She turned away. "I don't want to touch it. I don't care what it says."

"It could be important. How about I'll read it to you? Would that be okay?"

Kelsey shrugged. She knew she was being irrational. She should hear whatever James had to say. And Michael should hear it too. Let someone else be a witness to his insanity. "Okay," she said. "Read it."

Michael slipped his finger under the loosely sealed flap of the envelope and smoothed the letter open on his lap.

"*Dearest Kelsey,*" he read. "*By the time you read this, I will be gone. I had been planning to take you with me, my darling wife and light of my life, but I have come to understand that, while I love you with all my heart, you can never return that love.*

"*This is my fault. I stole what should have been freely given. I took what was never mine. Instead of earning your love and proving my worth, I crossed a line that should never be crossed. I can't undo what has been done. I perverted what should have been a beautiful thing. I hid behind the teachings of bullies, telling myself it was for your own good, and that you would come to love me in time.*

"*I know you probably can't understand this, but when I beat you*" — Michael's voice faltered as he read these words. He cleared his throat and continued — "*it was to teach you how to be an obedient wife. When I withheld food and comfort, it was to train you to behave in the fashion befitting a proper submissive woman.*"

Michael broke off, looking at Kelsey. "My god, the man is a raving lunatic. He's a monster. You poor girl." His voice cracked and Kelsey saw that tears were rolling down his cheeks. "Look, we don't have to read this now."

"No," Kelsey said, wanting Michael to hear what James had written, needing to hear it herself. He was, she realized, making a confession and a kind of apology, in his own twisted, sick way. "Keep going."

Michael took a breath, nodded and continued. "*I somehow managed to convince myself that you needed and even, on some level, wanted what I was doing to you. I suppressed my better nature, giving in to my baser instincts and lust without regard to your needs or desires.*

"Something happened this morning that finally cut through my already rattled defenses and made me see that I'd lost the very woman I claimed to love. I'd turned you into something you are not, and nearly snuffed out your soul in the process.

"I only pray you can recover. I don't ask for forgiveness, as I deserve none. I can promise you this. I will never darken your door again. I am going somewhere no one can follow, somewhere I can be at peace with what I have done.

"I love you. I'm sorry.

"James Matthew Bennett."

A sudden, urgent beeping sound startled Kelsey. She realized it was coming from a small walkie-talkie type device on Michael's belt. He stood and reached for it. "Police scanner," he explained as he pulled the device from his belt. "The beep tells me it's a local emergency."

"It's James," Kelsey said, no idea how she knew, but certain she was right.

Michael depressed the button on the device, and they listened to garbled voices. "Late model Audi A4...crashed headlong into the ravine." More unintelligible words and then, "Eyewitness says the car turned off and just drove right over the edge...Survivors unlikely..." Silence for several long seconds and then, "We're arriving at the scene...Holy cow, the car just exploded! Get backup here right away."

Kelsey stood and turned wordlessly to Michael. He held out his arms and she stepped into them. Leaning her cheek against his chest, she closed her eyes as he held her close.

"He finally let me go," she whispered, tears streaming down her face. "I'm free."

Epilogue

Michael Johansen thought he had seen it all in the nine years he'd been working, first as a cop and then as a private investigator specializing in missing persons. When Patrick and Katherine Rowan had enlisted his services and sent him up north to find their missing daughter, the local cops had been reasonably forthcoming with their files, though they hadn't managed to turn up much. When he'd interviewed her coworkers, one conversation in particular had stood out for him about James' apparently obsessive interest in Kelsey. Michael had learned to trust his gut, and his gut told him to follow that lead, in spite of the fact that James was supposedly off somewhere getting treatment for cancer.

His suspicions had been further stoked by Bennett's agitated and even hostile behavior during the interview. The timing had been too neat between Kelsey's disappearance and James' abrupt departure from the bank. And he remained the last person seen with Kelsey the night of her disappearance. Even so, Michael had known the odds were good that, with so many months behind them, Kelsey was probably long dead and buried. Still he'd hoped at least to discover what had happened and give her parents some closure.

The shock of finding Kelsey as quickly as he had, half-starved and terrified, had blinded him at first to her courage and inner strength. During the first couple of days when she'd been interviewed endlessly by the cops from her hospital bed, he had tried to keep his distance, at least emotionally, though in truth, he'd barely left her side. She had stabilized quickly and been released within a few days to return with her parents to their Florida home.

Even on that first day in the hospital before her parents had swooped in, he could see she'd begun to rally, refusing to be cast as the victim. Michael had admired that in her, aware the wounds she'd suffered went deeper than just the welts and marks that monster had left on her body. Michael had further admired her compassion in the face of what the police ruled as James' suicide. Even after what the man had put her through, she was sad for the way he'd ended his life.

Try as he might to resist it, Michael's attraction to Kelsey had been immediate and fierce, though he'd kept that firmly to himself. He knew she faced a long uphill battle to full recovery, and he certainly didn't intend to make things more complicated for her by coming on to her.

Yet once back in Florida, he couldn't seem to get the lovely young woman out of his head. He nearly called her a dozen times, but held himself back. He did check in with her parents after the first week, and had been gratified to learn she was doing well, all things considered. He'd told himself to let it go. He'd done his job and that was that. He was a professional. He would forget about her in time. He would throw himself into his work, as he always did, and forget the way she had felt in his arms, or the trusting look in her lovely green eyes.

He almost managed it.

Until the day she called him, and the sound of her sultry voice sent a jolt of pure joy right down to his toes.

~*~

Kelsey watched the waves rolling toward her and then falling back, their white caplets bubbling over the sand as the waves retreated. The sun was warm, the breeze softly scented with salt and suntan oil. She leaned back on her elbows and stared up at the wide blue sky. Closing her eyes, she became that soaring white bird she had metamorphosed into during the worst of her captivity, when to remain in her human form was just too painful.

She still had nightmares, waking in a cold sweat, shivering and sobbing, but they came less often now, and she was better able to shake off the shackles of the lingering dreams more quickly. The bruises and welts had all long since healed, save for the scar left from the bullet graze.

She thought sometimes of how James had called the marks left from the beatings "badges of courage", and how angrily she'd recoiled from that description at the time. Now, though, as she fingered the jagged scar left by the bullet, she wasn't so quick to dismiss the characterization. She had been alone and defenseless against someone much bigger and stronger than herself, but she had managed to get that gun, and would have shot him, too, if she'd had the chance. She'd slashed him with a kitchen knife, and she'd fully intended to kill him when she got the gun the second time, even though she'd been shaking like a leaf. She'd nearly been beaten down, but in the end she'd come alive again, ready to fight, never giving up.

"You can only be truly brave when you're afraid," she'd remembered reading somewhere, and it was true. She'd been terrified, but she'd been courageous, too. Still, even the bravest soul can only hold out so long when deprived of food, kept in chains and treated with a terrifying blend of brutality and kindness that had nearly driven her mad.

She had been on the edge of losing her mind, slipping each day a little deeper into the role James had so relentlessly forced her into—what he had called an obedient and submissive "wife". Under the guise of a stern but loving "husband", he had given free rein to his darkest fantasies, using the power of his position to twist the concept of love into something sharp and cutting, something that ripped into her soul and made her heart, as well as her body, bleed.

No wonder she had taken wing when she could, soaring away from whatever atrocity he was committing at the moment. It was during those times when she was sailing over a silent, deep blue sea on strong white wings that her mind somehow healed itself, at least a little, at least enough to keep the essence of who she was still alive somewhere beneath the brutalized, frightened girl she had become.

And yet, for all the evil James had done, she found she no longer hated him. They say that power corrupts, and absolute power corrupts absolutely, but in the end, James gave up that power. When he realized Michael was on the trail, he could have taken Kelsey and run, as he'd so carefully planned beforehand. But something, some lingering spark of humanity still burning inside him had flared long enough for him to commit one final, selfless act. He could have run, hiding forever in the shadows, always leaving Kelsey to wonder if someday, somehow, he would return to abduct her once again, this time taking her far away where no one could ever find her. Though his death had been tragic, knowing the nightmare was well and truly over let her sleep at night.

If Michael hadn't arrived when he had, showing James that photo from a family beach vacation and hinting that he knew more than he actually had, would Kelsey even now be held prisoner in a small house in some Mexican village, her mind finally destroyed by the constant barrage of torture, deprivation and brainwashing? The thought that James might have impregnated her during the week he'd withheld the birth control still made her shudder. Yet it had been the threat of bringing innocent babes into the nightmare world he'd created that had shaken her out of her torpor and given her the courage to fight. Even now, it was terrifying to realize just how close she'd come to losing everything, most especially herself.

Though the day was warm, she felt suddenly cold, as if icy fingers were scraping along her spine. She shuddered and pulled her knees up to her body, wrapping her arms around them.

A strong but gentle hand stroked her arm. "Hey, you okay?"

She turned to Michael, surprised when he wiped away a tear from her cheek with his thumb. She hadn't even realized she was crying.

During the first few months back in Florida with her parents, she would find herself sobbing uncontrollably at the drop of a hat, which had worried her parents to death, even when her therapist had assured them it was okay — it was just her mind and body's way of coping with pent-up stress as she worked through the trauma. Over time the stormy sob sessions had ebbed, yet there were still mornings she would wake up with a face wet with tears, or find herself quietly crying while reading a book or, as now, staring out at the ocean.

"Yeah." Kelsey smiled through the tears. Michael smiled back, his brilliant blue eyes crinkling at the corners. She liked it that he never minded when she cried. Even when it was bad, he would just hold her and stroke her hair. He never told her to stop, or that everything was fine now. He just let her *be*, and she loved him for it.

"I was just — remembering," she admitted.

"It's not something you're ever likely to forget." Michael turned his head to stare out at the water, though he kept his hand comfortingly on her arm. "But each day's a little easier."

"Yes," she agreed, leaning her body into his. He put his arm around her shoulders, and she leaned into him. Since the day she'd called him, Michael had been there as a friend, a constant support, a buffer between her and the press, the cops, even her parents, who meant well but had no idea how to cope with what had happened. He'd never rushed her, or made her feel obligated in any way for his steadfast, kind support.

Her therapist had warned her she might not be comfortable with a man for a long time, and might have some difficulty with intimacy as she worked through what had happened. She'd encouraged Kelsey to take her time before getting involved with anyone romantically. Kelsey had intended to take her advice. Michael, she had told herself over and over, was only a friend.

But as the days edged into weeks and slipped into months, Michael remained at her side, just a phone call away, always ready to take her to dinner, help her in her job search once she'd decided to remain in town to be near her parents, or just hang out and talk all night if that's what she needed at the time. And never once during all that time had he so much as tried to kiss her.

Until one night when it had just—happened. They were at her place—she'd finally convinced her parents she really needed a place of her own, especially now that she was becoming more firmly established at Peter Montage's art gallery. The job paid next to nothing, but thanks to the sizable stash of gold and cash James had left her, money really wasn't a consideration. At first it had been more about getting out and being around other people, but Kelsey had discovered she had an eye for good art. The gallery specialized in jewelry as art, and Kelsey loved combing the markets and craft fairs for undiscovered talent to bring to the gallery.

That particular Friday night, Michael and she were sharing a pizza and a bottle of wine at her place while watching some sappy movie. She had a nice buzz from the wine, and Michael looked incredibly handsome, his white linen shirt open at the throat to reveal the tufts of dark blond hair on his broad, muscular chest, his eyes sparking in the half-light of the television, his ash blond hair falling over his forehead.

She hadn't planned it, or even thought much about it at the time. She had just leaned over and kissed him, lightly, on the lips. After a moment, he had kissed her back. And then his arms had come around her, catching her in a warm but gentle embrace. It hadn't been awkward or weird, as she'd been afraid it might after all this time and all the sexual trauma she was still working through in therapy. It had just felt—right. Their mouths fit together, their bodies molding comfortably against each other as they stretched out along the sofa.

That first night they'd only kissed. She hadn't felt rushed by Michael, but nor had he treated her like some kind of fragile china doll that might break if he touched her, and she had been grateful for that.

When they finally did make love, some two weeks after that first sweet kiss, the connection was powerful and fierce, from both sides. Their bodies had melted together, and then melded together, as if they'd been waiting all their lives for precisely this moment in time. She had wanted him as much as he had wanted her, and for the first time in her nearly twenty-four years, she had understood what all the fuss was about.

"I was gonna save this till tonight when we go out for your birthday dinner, but..." Michael flashed a sudden, impish smile in her direction.

"What?" Kelsey twisted toward him with a grin. "Is it a present? I love presents."

"Well, it's just a little something I saw at a gallery in town..."

"You didn't." Michael had been snooping around the gallery for the past week, and she'd begun to suspect he had some ulterior motive beyond his claim he was just seeking the pleasure of her company.

"I did." Michael pulled an oblong jewelry box with a bedraggled satin bow tied inexpertly around it from beneath his towel. He held it out to her with a flourish. "Happy birthday, dear heart. I hope you like it."

Kelsey took the box in eager fingers and tugged at the bow. As she lifted the lid, her mouth fell open in surprise. "Michael," she breathed. "How did you...?" She looked up at him. "This isn't for sale. It's part of her private collection."

"I can be very persuasive," Michael replied with a straight face, though his blue eyes were dancing.

It was a piece by Lourdes Pablo, a local designer Kelsey had discovered at a craft show, whose exhibit at the gallery had taken the local art community by storm. Kelsey had greatly admired this particular bracelet, woven from strands of rose gold, copper and white gold, but had never dreamed it might be hers.

"Seriously, how did you get her to part with it?"

"It was simple. I told her it was your birthday."

"Wow, really?" Kelsey shook her head in wonderment.

"Really." Michael smiled that warm, kind smile of his that always made Kelsey feel cherished. "You may not realize it, Kelsey, but you've done a lot of very good things for a lot of people since you moved down here. If you hadn't discovered Lourdes and talked Peter into giving her a show, she might still be selling her beautiful work at crappy county fairs and flea markets. She was happy to part with it when she heard it was for you."

He reached for the box and Kelsey let him take it. He lifted out the delicately woven work of art, which glinted in the setting sun, and Kelsey held out her wrist. Michael slipped the clasp into place and Kelsey held out her arm to admire the beautiful bracelet.

"Thank you, Michael. This is the best present I ever got."

"I'm glad you like it, Kelsey. It reminds me of you—delicate, but strong."

Kelsey smiled, warmth moving through her. Michael leaned close and whispered suddenly, "Marry me, Kelsey. It doesn't have to be now, but someday, please, marry me. Say that you will?"

Kelsey turned her head so their noses were touching. Michael didn't pull away, and neither did she.

"I will," she replied, never more sure of anything in her life.

"Thank you, Kelsey." Michael grinned broadly. "That's the best present *I* ever got."

Available at Romance Unbound Publishing

(http://romanceunbound.com)

A Lover's Call
A Princely Gift
Accidental Slave
Alternative Treatment
Binding Discoveries
Blind Faith
Cast a Lover's Spell
Caught: Punished by Her Boss
Closely Held Secrets
Club de Sade
Confessions of a Submissive
Continuum of Desire
Dare to Dominate
Dream Master
Face of Submission
Finding Chandler
Forced Submission
Frog
Golden Angel
Golden Boy
Heart of Submission
Heart Thief
Island of Temptation
Jewel Thief

Julie's Submission
Lara's Submission
Masked Submission
Obsession: Girl Abducted
Odd Man Out
Perfect Cover
Pleasure Planet
Princess
Safe in Her Arms
Sarah's Awakening
Seduction of Colette
Slave Academy
Slave Castle
Slave Gamble
Slave Girl
Slave Island
Slave Jade
Sold into Slavery
Sub for Hire
Submission Times Two
Switch
Texas Surrender
The Abduction of Kelsey
The Auction
The Compound
The Cowboy Poet
The Master
The Solitary Knights of Pelham Bay
The Story of Owen
The Toy

Tough Boy
Tracy in Chains
True Kin Vampire Tales:
    Sacred Circle
    Outcast
    Sacred Blood
True Submission
Two Loves for Alex
Two Masters for Alexis
Wicked Hearts

Connect with Claire

Website: http://clairethompson.net
Romance Unbound Publishing: http://romanceunbound.com
Twitter: http://twitter.com/CThompsonAuthor
Facebook: http://www.facebook.com/ClaireThompsonauthor

Made in the USA
San Bernardino, CA
11 June 2016